The Little Foxes
and
Another Part of the Forest

Books by Lillian Hellman

PLAYS

The Children's Hour (1934)
Days to Come (1936)
The Little Foxes (1939)
Watch on the Rhine (1941)
The Searching Wind (1944)
Another Part of the Forest (1947)
Montserrat (an adaptation, 1950)
The Autumn Garden (1951)
The Lark (an adaptation, 1956)
Candide (an operetta, 1957)
Toys in the Attic (1960)
My Mother, My Father and Me (an adaptation, 1963)
The Collected Plays (1972)

MEMOIRS

An Unfinished Woman (1969)
Pentimento (1973)

EDITED BY LILLIAN HELLMAN

The Selected Letters of Anton Chekhov (1955)
The Big Knockover: Stories and Short Novels by Dashiell Hammett (1966)

The Little Foxes

and

Another Part of the Forest

Two Plays by

Lillian Hellman

The Viking Press | New York

Viking Compass Edition
issued in 1973 by The Viking Press, Inc.
625 Madison Avenue, New York, N.Y. 10022
Distributed in Canada by
The Macmillan Company of Canada Limited
SBN 670-00394-8
Library of Congress catalog card number: 73-8034

The Little Foxes published by agreement with Random House, Inc.

Contents

The Little Foxes

For ARTHUR KOBER *and* LOUIS KRONENBERGER
who have been my good friends

"Take us the foxes, the little foxes,
that spoil the vines;
for our vines have tender grapes."

The Little Foxes was first produced at the National Theatre, New York City, on February 15, 1939, with the following cast:

In order of appearance

Addie	ABBIE MITCHELL
Cal	JOHN MARRIOTT
Birdie Hubbard	PATRICIA COLLINGE
Oscar Hubbard	CARL BENTON REID
Leo Hubbard	DAN DURYEA
Regina Giddens	TALLULAH BANKHEAD
William Marshall	LEE BAKER
Benjamin Hubbard	CHARLES DINGLE
Alexandra Giddens	FLORENCE WILLIAMS
Horace Giddens	FRANK CONROY

Produced and staged by HERMAN SHUMLIN

Settings designed by HOWARD BAY

Costumes designed by ALINE BERNSTEIN

The scene of the play is the living room of the Giddens house, in a small town in the South.

ACT ONE: The Spring of 1900, evening.

ACT TWO: A week later, early morning.

ACT THREE: Two weeks later, late afternoon.

There has been no attempt to write Southern dialect. It is to be understood that the accents are Southern.

Act One

SCENE: *The living room of the Giddens house, in a small town in the deep South, the Spring of 1900. Upstage is a staircase leading to the second story. Upstage, right, are double doors to the dining room. When these doors are open we see a section of the dining room and the furniture. Upstage, left, is an entrance hall with a coat-rack and umbrella stand. There are large lace-curtained windows on the left wall. The room is lit by a center gas chandelier and painted china oil lamps on the tables. Against the wall is a large piano. Downstage, right, are a high couch, a large table, several chairs. Against the left back wall are a table and several chairs. Near the window there are a smaller couch and tables. The room is good-looking, the furniture expensive; but it reflects no particular taste. Everything is of the best and that is all.*

AT RISE: ADDIE, *a tall, nice-looking Negro woman of about fifty-five, is closing the windows. From behind the closed dining-room doors there is the sound of voices. After a second,* CAL, *a middle-aged Negro, comes in from the entrance hall carrying a tray with glasses and a bottle of port.* ADDIE *crosses, takes the tray from him, puts it on table, begins to arrange it.*

ADDIE

(*Pointing to the bottle*)

You gone stark out of your head?

CAL

No, smart lady, I ain't. Miss Regina told me to get out that bottle. (*Points to bottle*) That very bottle for the mighty honored guest. When Miss Regina changes orders like that you can bet your dime she got her reason.

ADDIE

(*Points to dining room*)

Go on. You'll be needed.

CAL

Miss Zan she had two helpings frozen fruit cream and she tell that honored guest, she tell him that you make the best frozen fruit cream in all the South.

ADDIE

(*Smiles, pleased*)

Did she? Well, see that Belle saves a little for her. She like it right before she go to bed. Save a few little cakes, too, she like—

(*The dining-room doors are opened and quickly closed again by* BIRDIE HUBBARD. BIRDIE *is a woman of about forty, with a pretty, well-bred, faded face. Her movements are usually nervous and timid, but now, as she comes running into the room, she is gay and excited.* CAL *turns to* BIRDIE.)

BIRDIE

Oh, Cal. (*Closes door*) I want you to get one of the kitchen boys to run home for me. He's to look in my desk drawer and— (*To* ADDIE) My, Addie. What a good supper! Just as good as good can be.

ADDIE

You look pretty this evening, Miss Birdie, and young.

BIRDIE

(*Laughing*)

Me, young? (*Turns back to* CAL) Maybe you better find Simon and tell him to do it himself. He's to look in my desk, the left drawer, and bring my music album right away. Mr. Marshall is very anxious to see it because of his father and the opera in Chicago. (*To* ADDIE) Mr. Marshall is such a polite man with his manners and very educated and cultured and I've told him all about how my mama and papa used to go to Europe for the music— (*Laughs. To* ADDIE) Imagine going all the way to Europe just to listen to music. Wouldn't that be nice, Addie? Just to sit there and listen and— (*Turns and steps to* CAL) *Left* drawer, Cal. Tell him that twice because he forgets. And tell him not to let any of the things drop out of the album and to bring it right in here when he comes back.

(*The dining-room doors are opened and quickly closed by* OSCAR HUBBARD. *He is a man in his late forties.*)

CAL

Yes'm. But Simon he won't get it right. But I'll tell him.

BIRDIE

Left drawer, Cal, and tell him to bring the blue book and—

OSCAR

(*Sharply*)

Birdie.

BIRDIE

(*Turning nervously*)

Oh, Oscar. I was just sending Simon for my music album.

OSCAR

(*To* CAL)

Never mind about the album. Miss Birdie has changed her mind.

BIRDIE

But, really, Oscar. Really I promised Mr. Marshall. I—

(CAL *looks at them, exits.*)

OSCAR

Why do you leave the dinner table and go running about like a child?

BIRDIE

(*Trying to be gay*)

But, Oscar, Mr. Marshall said most specially he *wanted* to see my album. I told him about the time Mama met Wagner, and Mrs. Wagner gave her the signed program and the big picture. Mr. Marshall wants to see that. Very, very much. We had such a nice talk and—

OSCAR

(*Taking a step to her*)

You have been chattering to him like a magpie. You haven't let him be for a second. I can't think he came South to be bored with you.

BIRDIE

(*Quickly, hurt*)

He wasn't bored. I don't believe he was bored. He's a very

educated, cultured gentleman. (*Her voice rises*) I just don't believe it. You always talk like that when I'm having a nice time.

OSCAR

(*Turning to her, sharply*)

You have had too much wine. Get yourself in hand now.

BIRDIE

(*Drawing back, about to cry, shrilly*)

What am I doing? I am not doing anything. What am I doing?

OSCAR

(*Taking a step to her, tensely*)

I said get yourself in hand. Stop acting like a fool.

BIRDIE

(*Turns to him, quietly*)

I don't believe he was bored. I just don't believe it. Some people like music and like to talk about it. That's all I was doing.

(LEO HUBBARD *comes hurrying through the dining-room door. He is a young man of twenty, with a weak kind of good looks.*)

LEO

Mama! Papa! They are coming in now.

OSCAR

(*Softly*)

Sit down, Birdie. Sit down now. (BIRDIE *sits down, bows her head as if to hide her face.*)

(*The dining-room doors are opened by* CAL. *We see people beginning to rise from the table.* REGINA GIDDENS *comes in with* WILLIAM MARSHALL. REGINA *is a handsome woman of forty.* MARSHALL *is forty-five, pleasant-looking, self-possessed. Behind them comes* ALEXANDRA GIDDENS, *a very pretty, rather delicate-looking girl of seventeen. She is followed by* BENJAMIN HUBBARD, *fifty-five, with a large jovial face and the light graceful movements that one often finds in large men.*)

REGINA

Mr. Marshall, I think you're trying to console me. Chicago may be the noisiest, dirtiest city in the world but I should still prefer it to the sound of our horses and the smell of our azaleas. I should like crowds of people, and theatres, and lovely women— *Very* lovely women, Mr. Marshall?

MARSHALL

(*Crossing to sofa*)

In Chicago? Oh, I suppose so. But I can tell you this: I've never dined there with three *such* lovely ladies.

(ADDIE *begins to pass the port.*)

BEN

Our Southern women are well favored.

LEO

(*Laughs*)

But one must go to Mobile for the ladies, sir. Very elegant worldly ladies, too.

BEN

(*Looks at him very deliberately*)

Worldly, eh? *Worldly,* did you say?

OSCAR

(*Hastily, to* LEO)

Your uncle Ben means that worldliness is not a mark of beauty in any woman.

LEO

(*Quickly*)

Of course, Uncle Ben. I didn't mean—

MARSHALL

Your port is excellent, Mrs. Giddens.

REGINA

Thank you, Mr. Marshall. We had been saving that bottle, hoping we could open it just for you.

ALEXANDRA

(*As* ADDIE *comes to her with the tray*)

Oh. May I *really,* Addie?

ADDIE

Better ask Mama.

ALEXANDRA

May I, Mama?

REGINA

(*Nods, smiles*)

In Mr. Marshall's honor.

ALEXANDRA

(*Smiles*)

Mr. Marshall, this will be the first taste of port I've ever had.

(ADDIE *serves* LEO.)

MARSHALL

No one ever had their first taste of a better port. (*He lifts his glass in a toast; she lifts hers; they both drink*) Well, I suppose it is all true, Mrs. Giddens.

REGINA

What is true?

MARSHALL

That you Southerners occupy a unique position in America. You live better than the rest of us, you eat better, you drink better. I wonder you find time, or want to find time, to do business.

BEN

A great many Southerners don't.

MARSHALL

Do all of you live here together?

REGINA

Here with me? (*Laughs*) Oh, no. My brother Ben lives next door. My brother Oscar and his family live in the next square.

BEN

But we are a very close family. We've always *wanted* it that way.

MARSHALL

That is very pleasant. Keeping your family together to share each other's lives. My family moves around too much. My children seem never to come home. Away at school in the winter; in the summer, Europe with their mother—

REGINA

(*Eagerly*)

Oh, yes. Even down here we read about Mrs. Marshall in the society pages.

MARSHALL

I dare say. She moves about a great deal. And all of you are part of the same business? Hubbard Sons?

BEN

(*Motions to* OSCAR)

Oscar and me. (*Motions to* REGINA) My sister's good husband is a banker.

MARSHALL

(*Looks at* REGINA, *surprised*)

Oh.

REGINA

I am so sorry that my husband isn't here to meet you. He's been very ill. He is at Johns Hopkins. But he will be home soon. We think he is getting better now.

LEO

I work for Uncle Horace. (REGINA *looks at him*) I mean I work for Uncle Horace at his bank. I keep an eye on things while he's away.

REGINA

(*Smiles*)

Really, Leo?

BEN

(*Looks at* LEO, *then to* MARSHALL)

Modesty in the young is as excellent as it is rare. (*Looks at* LEO *again.*)

OSCAR

(*To* LEO)

Your uncle means that a young man should speak more modestly.

LEO

(*Hastily, taking a step to* BEN)

Oh, I didn't mean, sir—

MARSHALL

Oh, Mrs. Hubbard. Where's that Wagner autograph you promised to let me see? My train will be leaving soon and—

BIRDIE

The autograph? Oh. Well. Really, Mr. Marshall, I didn't mean to chatter so about it. Really I— (*Nervously, looking at* OSCAR) You must excuse me. I didn't get it because, well, because I had—I—I had a little headache and—

OSCAR

My wife is a miserable victim of headaches.

REGINA

(*Quickly*)

Mr. Marshall said at supper that he would like you to play for him, Alexandra.

ALEXANDRA

(*Who has been looking at* BIRDIE)

It's not I who play well, sir. It's my aunt. She plays just wonderfully. She's my teacher. (*Rises. Eagerly*) May we play a duet? May we, Mama?

BIRDIE

(*Taking* ALEXANDRA'S *hand*)

Thank you, dear. But I have my headache now. I—

OSCAR

(*Sharply*)

Don't be stubborn, Birdie. Mr. Marshall wants you to play.

MARSHALL

Indeed I do. If your headache isn't—

BIRDIE

(*Hesitates, then gets up, pleased*)

But I'd like to, sir. Very much. (*She and* ALEXANDRA *go to the piano.*)

MARSHALL

It's very remarkable how you Southern aristocrats have kept together. Kept together and kept what belonged to you.

BEN

You misunderstand, sir. Southern aristocrats have *not* kept together and have *not* kept what belonged to them.

MARSHALL

(*Laughs, indicates room*)

You don't call this keeping what belongs to you?

BEN

But we are not aristocrats. (*Points to* BIRDIE *at the piano*) Our brother's wife is the only one of us who belongs to the Southern aristocracy.

(BIRDIE *looks towards* BEN.)

MARSHALL

(*Smiles*)

My information is that you people have been here, and solidly here, for a long time.

OSCAR

And so we have. Since our great-grandfather.

BEN

(*Smiles*)

Who was *not* an aristocrat, like Birdie's.

MARSHALL

(*A little sharply*)

You make great distinctions.

BEN

Oh, they have been made for us. And maybe they are important distinctions. (*Leans forward, intimately*) Now you take Birdie's family. When my great-grandfather came here they were the highest-tone plantation owners in this state.

LEO

(*Steps to* MARSHALL. *Proudly*)

My mother's grandfather was *governor* of the state before the war.

OSCAR

They owned the plantation, Lionnet. You may have heard of it, sir?

MARSHALL

(*Laughs*)

No, I've never heard of anything but brick houses on a lake, and cotton mills.

BEN

Lionnet in its day was the best cotton land in the South. It still brings us in a fair crop. (*Sits back*) Ah, they were great days for those people—even when I can remember. They had the best of everything. (BIRDIE *turns to them*) Cloth from Paris, trips to Europe, horses you can't raise any more, niggers to lift their fingers—

BIRDIE

(*Suddenly*)

We were good to our people. Everybody knew that. We were better to them than—

(MARSHALL *looks up at* BIRDIE.)

REGINA

Why, Birdie. You aren't playing.

BEN

But when the war comes these fine gentlemen ride off and leave the cotton, *and* the women, to rot.

BIRDIE

My father was killed in the war. He was a fine soldier, Mr. Marshall. A fine man.

REGINA

Oh, certainly, Birdie. A famous soldier.

BEN

(*To* BIRDIE)

But that isn't the tale I am telling Mr. Marshall. (*To* MARSHALL) Well, sir, the war ends. (BIRDIE *goes back to piano*) Lionnet is almost ruined, and the sons finish ruining it. And there were thousands like them. Why? (*Leans forward*) Because the Southern aristocrat can adapt himself to nothing. Too high-tone to try.

MARSHALL

Sometimes it is difficult to learn new ways. (BIRDIE *and* ALEXANDRA *begin to play.* MARSHALL *leans forward, listening.*)

BEN

Perhaps, perhaps. (*He sees that* MARSHALL *is listening to the music. Irritated, he turns to* BIRDIE *and* ALEXANDRA *at the piano, then back to* MARSHALL) You're right, Mr. Marshall. It is difficult to learn new ways. But maybe that's why it's profitable. *Our* grandfather and *our* father learned the new ways and learned how to make them pay. They work. (*Smiles nastily*) *They* are in trade. Hubbard Sons, Merchandise. Others, Birdie's family, for example, look down on them. (*Settles back in chair*) To make a long story short, Lionnet now belongs to *us.* (BIRDIE *stops playing*) Twenty years ago we took over their land, their cotton, and their daughter. (BIRDIE *rises and stands stiffly by the piano.* MARSHALL, *who has been watching her, rises.*)

MARSHALL

May I bring you a glass of port, Mrs. Hubbard?

BIRDIE

(*Softly*)

No, thank you, sir. You are most polite.

REGINA

(*Sharply, to* BEN)

You are boring Mr. Marshall with these ancient family tales.

BEN

I hope not. I hope not. I am trying to make an important point— (*Bows to* MARSHALL) for our future business partner.

OSCAR

(*To* MARSHALL)

My brother always says that it's folks like us who have struggled and fought to bring to our land some of the prosperity of your land.

BEN

Some people call that patriotism.

REGINA

(*Laughs gaily*)

I hope you don't find my brothers too obvious, Mr. Marshall. I'm afraid they mean that this is the time for the ladies to leave the gentlemen to talk business.

MARSHALL

(*Hastily*)

Not at all. We settled everything this afternoon. (MARSHALL *looks at his watch*) I have only a few minutes before I must leave for the train. (*Smiles at her*) And I insist they be spent with you.

REGINA

And with another glass of port.

MARSHALL

Thank you.

BEN

(*To* REGINA)

My sister is right. (*To* MARSHALL) I am a plain man and I am trying to say a plain thing. A man ain't only in business for what he can get out of it. It's got to give him something here. (*Puts hand to his breast*) That's every bit as true for the nigger picking cotton for a silver quarter, as it is for you and me. (REGINA *gives* MARSHALL *a glass of port*) If it don't give him something here, then he don't pick the cotton right. Money isn't all. Not by three shots.

MARSHALL

Really? Well, I always thought it was a great deal.

REGINA

And so did I, Mr. Marshall.

MARSHALL

(*Leans forward. Pleasantly, but with meaning*)

Now you don't have to convince me that you are the right

people for the deal. I wouldn't be here if you hadn't convinced me six months ago. You want the mill here, and I want it here. It isn't my business to find out *why* you want it.

BEN

To bring the machine to the cotton, and not the cotton to the machine.

MARSHALL

(*Amused*)

You have a turn for neat phrases, Hubbard. Well, however grand your reasons are, mine are simple: I want to make money and I believe I'll make it on you. (*As* BEN *starts to speak, he smiles*) Mind you, I have no objections to more high-minded reasons. They are mighty valuable in business. It's fine to have partners who so closely follow the teachings of Christ. (*Gets up*) And now I must leave for my train.

REGINA

I'm sorry you won't stay over with us, Mr. Marshall, but you'll come again. Any time you like.

BEN

(*Motions to* LEO, *indicating the bottle*)

Fill them up, boy, fill them up. (LEO *moves around filling the glasses as* BEN *speaks*) Down here, sir, we have a strange custom. We drink the *last* drink for a toast. That's to prove that the Southerner is always still on his feet for the last drink. (*Picks up his glass*) It was Henry Frick, your Mr. Henry Frick, who said, "Railroads are the Rembrandts of investments." Well, *I* say, "Southern cotton mills *will be* the Rembrandts of investment." So I give you the firm of Hubbard Sons and Marshall, Cotton Mills, and to it a long and prosperous life.

(*They all pick up their glasses.* MARSHALL *looks at them, amused. Then he, too, lifts his glass, smiles.*)

OSCAR

The children will drive you to the depot. Leo! Alexandra! You will drive Mr. Marshall down.

LEO

(*Eagerly, looks at* BEN *who nods*)

Yes, sir. (*To* MARSHALL) Not often Uncle Ben lets *me* drive the horses. And a beautiful pair they are. (*Starts for hall*) Come on, Zan.

ALEXANDRA

May I drive tonight, Uncle Ben, please? I'd like to and—

BEN

(*Shakes his head, laughs*)

In your evening clothes? Oh, no, my dear.

ALEXANDRA

But Leo always— (*Stops, exits quickly.*)

REGINA

I don't like to say good-bye to you, Mr. Marshall.

MARSHALL

Then we won't say good-bye. You have promised that you would come and let me show you Chicago. Do I have to make you promise again?

REGINA

(*Looks at him as he presses her hand*)

I promise again.

MARSHALL

(*Touches her hand again, then moves to* BIRDIE)

Good-bye, Mrs. Hubbard.

BIRDIE

(*Shyly, with sweetness and dignity*)

Good-bye, sir.

MARSHALL

(*As he passes* REGINA)

Remember.

REGINA

I will.

OSCAR

We'll see you to the carriage.

(MARSHALL *exits, followed by* BEN *and* OSCAR. *For a second* REGINA *and* BIRDIE *stand looking after them. Then* REGINA *throws up her arms, laughs happily.*)

REGINA

And there, Birdie, goes the man who has opened the door to our future.

BIRDIE

(*Surprised at the unaccustomed friendliness*)

What?

REGINA

(*Turning to her*)

Our future. Yours and mine, Ben's and Oscar's, the children— (*Looks at* BIRDIE's *puzzled face, laughs*) Our future! (*Gaily*) You were charming at supper, Birdie. Mr. Marshall certainly thought so.

BIRDIE

(*Pleased*)

Why, Regina! Do you think he did?

REGINA

Can't you tell when you're being admired?

BIRDIE

Oscar said I bored Mr. Marshall. (*Then quietly*) But he admired *you*. He told me so.

REGINA

What did he say?

BIRDIE

He said to me, "I hope your sister-in-law will come to Chicago. Chicago will be at her feet." He said the ladies would bow to your manners and the gentlemen to your looks.

REGINA

Did he? He seems a lonely man. Imagine being lonely with all that money. I don't think he likes his wife.

BIRDIE

Not like his wife? What a thing to say.

REGINA

She's away a great deal. He said that several times. And once he made fun of her being so social and high-tone. But that fits in all right. (*Sits back, arms on back of sofa, stretches*) Her being social, I mean. She can introduce me. It won't take long with an introduction from her.

BIRDIE

(*Bewildered*)

Introduce you? In Chicago? You mean you really might go? Oh, Regina, you can't leave here. What about Horace?

REGINA

Don't look so scared about everything, Birdie. I'm going to live in Chicago. I've always wanted to. And now there'll be plenty of money to go with.

BIRDIE

But Horace won't be able to move around. You know what the doctor wrote.

REGINA

There'll be millions, Birdie, millions. You know what I've always said when people told me we were rich? I said I think you should either be a nigger or a millionaire. In between, like us, what for? (*Laughs. Looks at* BIRDIE) But I'm not going away tomorrow, Birdie. There's plenty of time to worry about Horace when he comes home. If he ever decides to come home.

BIRDIE

Will we be going to Chicago? I mean, Oscar and Leo and me?

REGINA

You? I shouldn't think so. (*Laughs*) Well, we must remember tonight. It's a very important night and we mustn't forget it. We shall plan all the things we'd like to have and then we'll really have them. Make a wish, Birdie, any wish. It's bound to come true now.

(BEN *and* OSCAR *enter.*)

BIRDIE

(*Laughs*)

Well. Well, I don't know. Maybe. (REGINA *turns to look at* BEN) Well, I guess I'd know right off what I wanted.

(OSCAR *stands by the upper window, waves to the departing carriage.*)

REGINA

(*Looks up at* BEN, *smiles. He smiles back at her*)

Well, you did it.

BEN

Looks like it might be we did.

REGINA

(*Springs up, laughs*)

Looks like it! Don't pretend. You're like a cat who's been licking the cream. (*Crosses to wine bottle*) Now we must all have a drink to celebrate.

OSCAR

The children, Alexandra and Leo, make a very handsome couple, Regina. Marshall remarked himself what fine young folks they were. How well they looked together!

REGINA

(*Sharply*)

Yes. You said that before, Oscar.

BEN

Yes, sir. It's beginning to look as if the deal's all set. I may not be a subtle man—but— (*Turns to them. After a second*) Now somebody ask me how I know the deal is set.

OSCAR

What do you mean, Ben?

BEN

You remember I told him that down here we drink the *last* drink for a toast?

OSCAR

(*Thoughtfully*)

Yes. I never heard that before.

BEN

Nobody's ever heard it before. God forgives those who invent what they need. I already had his signature. But we've all done business with men whose word over a glass is better than a bond. Anyway it don't hurt to have both.

OSCAR

(*Turns to* REGINA)

You understand what Ben means?

REGINA

(*Smiles*)

Yes, Oscar. I understand. I understood immediately.

BEN

(*Looks at her admiringly*)

Did you, Regina? Well, when he lifted his glass to drink, I closed my eyes and saw the bricks going into place.

REGINA

And *I* saw a lot more than that.

BEN

Slowly, slowly. As yet we have only our hopes.

REGINA

Birdie and I have just been planning what we want. I know what I want. What will you want, Ben?

BEN

Caution. Don't count the chickens. (*Leans back, laughs*) Well, God would allow us a little daydreaming. Good for the soul when you've worked hard enough to deserve it. (*Pauses*) I think I'll have a stable. For a long time I've had my good eyes on Carter's in Savannah. A rich man's pleasure, the sport of kings, why not the sport of Hubbards? Why not?

REGINA

(*Smiles*)

Why not? What will you have, Oscar?

OSCAR

I don't know. (*Thoughtfully*) The pleasure of seeing the bricks grow will be enough for me.

BEN

Oh, of course. Our *greatest* pleasure will be to see the bricks grow. But we are all entitled to a little side indulgence.

OSCAR

Yes, I suppose so. Well, then, I think we might take a few trips here and there, eh, Birdie?

BIRDIE

(*Surprised at being consulted*)

Yes, Oscar. I'd like that.

OSCAR

We might even make a regular trip to Jekyll Island. I've heard the Cornelly place is for sale. We might think about buying it. Make a nice change. Do you good, Birdie, a change of climate. Fine shooting on Jekyll, the best.

BIRDIE

I'd like—

OSCAR

(*Indulgently*)

What would you like?

BIRDIE

Two things. Two things I'd like most.

REGINA

Two! I should like a thousand. You are modest, Birdie.

BIRDIE

(*Warmly, delighted with the unexpected interest*)

I should like to have Lionnet back. I know you own it now, but I'd like to see it fixed up again, the way Mama and Papa had it. Every year it used to get a nice coat of paint—Papa was very particular about the paint—and the lawn was so smooth all the way down to the river, with the trims of zinnias and red-feather plush. And the figs and blue little plums and the scuppernongs— (*Smiles. Turns to* REGINA) The organ is still there and it wouldn't cost much to fix. We could have parties for Zan, the way Mama used to have for me.

BEN

That's a pretty picture, Birdie. Might be a most pleasant way to live. (*Dismissing* BIRDIE) What do you want, Regina?

BIRDIE

(*Very happily, not noticing that they are no longer listening to her*)

I could have a cutting garden. Just where Mama's used to be. Oh, I do think we could be happier there. Papa used to say that *nobody* had ever lost their temper at Lionnet, and *nobody* ever would. Papa would never let anybody be nasty-spoken or mean. No, sir. He just didn't like it.

BEN

What do you want, Regina?

REGINA

I'm going to Chicago. And when I'm settled there and know the right people and the right things to buy—because I certainly don't now—I shall go to Paris and buy them. (*Laughs*) I'm going to leave you and Oscar to count the bricks.

BIRDIE

Oscar. Please let me have Lionnet back.

OSCAR

(*To* REGINA)

You are serious about moving to Chicago?

BEN

She is going to see the great world and leave us in the little one. Well, we'll come and visit you and meet all the great and be proud to think you are our sister.

REGINA

(*Gaily*)

Certainly. And you won't even have to learn to be subtle, Ben. Stay as you are. You will be rich and the rich don't have to be subtle.

OSCAR

But what about Alexandra? She's seventeen. Old enough to be thinking about marrying.

BIRDIE

And, Oscar, I have one more wish. Just one more wish.

OSCAR

(*Turns*)

What is it, Birdie? What are you saying?

BIRDIE

I want you to stop shooting. I mean, so much. I don't like to see animals and birds killed just for the killing. You only throw them away—

BEN

(*To* REGINA)

It'll take a great deal of money to live as you're planning, Regina.

REGINA

Certainly. But there'll be plenty of money. You have estimated the profits very high.

BEN

I have—

BIRDIE

(OSCAR *is looking at her furiously*)

And you never let anybody else shoot, and the niggers need it so much to keep from starving. It's wicked to shoot food just because you like to shoot, when poor people need it so—

BEN

(*Laughs*)

I have estimated the profits very high—for myself.

REGINA

What did you say?

BIRDIE

I've always wanted to speak about it, Oscar.

OSCAR

(*Slowly, carefully*)

What are you chattering about?

BIRDIE

(*nervously*)

I was talking about Lionnet and—and about your shooting—

OSCAR

You are exciting yourself.

REGINA

(*To* BEN)

I didn't hear you. There was so much talking.

OSCAR

(*To* BIRDIE)

You have been acting very childish, very excited, all evening.

BIRDIE

Regina asked me what I'd like.

REGINA

What did you say, Ben?

BIRDIE

Now that we'll be so rich everybody was saying what they would like, so *I* said what *I* would like, too.

BEN

I said— (*He is interrupted by* OSCAR.)

OSCAR

(*To* BIRDIE)

Very well. We've all heard you. That's enough now.

BEN

I am waiting. (*They stop*) I am waiting for you to finish. You and Birdie. Four conversations are three too many. (BIRDIE *slowly sits down.* BEN *smiles, to* REGINA) I said that I had, and I do, estimate the profits very high—for myself, and Oscar, of course.

REGINA

(*Slowly*)

And what does that mean?

(BEN *shrugs, looks towards* OSCAR.)

OSCAR

(*Looks at* BEN, *clears throat*)

Well, Regina, it's like this. For forty-nine per cent Marshall will put up four hundred thousand dollars. For fifty-one per cent— (*Smiles archly*) a controlling interest, mind you, we will put up two hundred and twenty-five thousand dollars besides offering him certain benefits that our (*looks at* BEN) local position allows us to manage. Ben means that two hundred and twenty-five thousand dollars is a lot of money.

REGINA

I know the terms and I know it's a lot of money.

BEN

(*Nodding*)

It is.

OSCAR

Ben means that we are ready with our two-thirds of the money. Your third, Horace's I mean, doesn't seem to be ready. (*Raises his hand as* REGINA *starts to speak*) Ben has written to Horace, I have written, and you have written. He answers. But he never mentions this business. Yet we have explained it to him in great detail, and told him the urgency. Still he never mentions it. Ben has been very patient, Regina. Naturally, you are our sister and we want you to benefit from anything we do.

REGINA

And in addition to your concern for me, you do not want control to go out of the family. (*To* BEN) That right, Ben?

BEN

That's cynical. (*Smiles*) Cynicism is an unpleasant way of saying the truth.

OSCAR

No need to be cynical. We'd have no trouble raising the third share, the share that you want to take.

REGINA

I am sure you could get the third share, the share you were saving for me. But that would give you a strange partner. And strange partners sometimes want a great deal. (*Smiles unpleasantly*) But perhaps it would be wise for you to find him.

OSCAR

Now, now. Nobody says we *want* to do that. We would like to have you in and you would like to come in.

REGINA

Yes. I certainly would.

BEN

(*Laughs, puts up his hand*)

But we haven't heard from Horace.

REGINA

I've given my word that Horace will put up the money. That should be enough.

BEN

Oh, it was enough. I took your word. But I've got to have more than your word now. The contracts will be signed this week, and Marshall will want to see our money soon after. Regina, Horace has been in Baltimore for five months. I know that you've written him to come home, and that he hasn't come.

OSCAR

It's beginning to look as if he doesn't want to come home.

REGINA

Of course he wants to come home. You can't move around with heart trouble at any moment you choose. You know what doctors are like once they get their hands on a case like this—

OSCAR

They can't very well keep him from answering letters, can they? (REGINA *turns to* BEN) They couldn't keep him from arranging for the money if he wanted to—

REGINA

Has it occurred to you that Horace is also a good business man?

BEN

Certainly. He is a shrewd trader. Always has been. The bank is proof of that.

REGINA

Then, possibly, he may be keeping silent because he doesn't think he is getting enough for his money. (*Looks at* OSCAR) Seventy-five thousand he has to put up. That's a lot of money, too.

OSCAR

Nonsense. He knows a good thing when he hears it. He knows that we can make *twice* the profit on cotton goods manufactured *here* than can be made in the North.

BEN

That isn't what Regina means. (*Smiles*) May I interpret you, Regina? (*To* OSCAR) Regina is saying that Horace wants *more* than a third of our share.

OSCAR

But he's only putting up a third of the money. You put up a third and you get a third. What else *could* he expect?

REGINA

Well, *I* don't know. I don't know about these things. It would seem that if you put up a third you should only get a third. But then again, there's no law about it, is there? I should think that if you knew your money was very badly needed, well, you just might say, I want more, I want a bigger share. You boys have done that. I've heard you say so.

BEN

(*After a pause, laughs*)

So you believe he has deliberately held out? For a larger share? (*Leaning forward*) Well, I *don't* believe it. But I *do* believe that's what *you* want. Am I right, Regina?

REGINA

Oh, I shouldn't like to be too definite. But I *could* say that I wouldn't like to persuade Horace unless he did get a larger share. I must look after his interests. It seems only natural—

OSCAR

And where would the larger share come from?

REGINA

I don't know. That's not my business. (*Giggles*) But perhaps it could come off your share, Oscar.

(REGINA *and* BEN *laugh.*)

OSCAR

(*Rises and wheels furiously on both of them as they laugh*) What kind of talk is this?

BEN

I haven't said a thing.

OSCAR

(*To* REGINA)

You are talking very big tonight.

REGINA

(*Stops laughing*)

Am I? Well, you should know me well enough to know that I wouldn't be asking for things I didn't think I could get.

OSCAR

Listen. I don't believe you can even get Horace to come home, much less get money from him or talk quite so big about what you want.

REGINA

Oh, I can get him home.

OSCAR

Then why haven't you?

REGINA

I thought I should fight his battles for him, before he came home. Horace is a very sick man. And even if *you* don't care how sick he is, I do.

BEN

Stop this foolish squabbling. How can you get him home?

REGINA

I will send Alexandra to Baltimore. She will ask him to come home. She will say that she *wants* him to come home, and that *I* want him to come home.

BIRDIE

(*Suddenly*)

Well, of course she wants him here, but he's sick and maybe he's happy where he is.

REGINA

(*Ignores* BIRDIE, *to* BEN)

You agree that he will come home if she asks him to, if she says that I miss him and want him—

BEN

(*Looks at her, smiles*)

I admire you, Regina. And I agree. That's settled now and— (*Starts to rise.*)

REGINA

(*Quickly*)

But before she brings him home, I want to know what he's going to get.

BEN

What do you want?

REGINA

Twice what you offered.

BEN

Well, you won't get it.

OSCAR

(*To* REGINA)

I think you've gone crazy.

REGINA

I don't want to fight, Ben—

BEN

I don't either. You won't get it. There isn't any chance of that. (*Roguishly*) You're holding us up, and that's not pretty, Regina, not pretty. (*Holds up his hand as he sees she is about to speak*) But we need you, and I don't want to fight. Here's what I'll do: I'll give Horace forty per cent, instead of the thirty-three and a third he really should get. I'll do that, provided he is home and his money is up within two weeks. How's that?

REGINA

All right.

OSCAR

I've asked before: where is this extra share coming from?

BEN

(*Pleasantly*)

From you. From your share.

OSCAR

(*Furiously*)

From me, is it? That's just fine and dandy. That's my reward. For thirty-five years I've worked my hands to the bone for you. For thirty-five years I've done all the things you didn't want to do. And this is what I—

BEN

(*Turns slowly to look at* OSCAR. OSCAR *breaks off*)

My, my. I am being attacked tonight on all sides. First by my sister, then by my brother. And I ain't a man who likes being attacked. I can't believe that God wants the strong to parade their strength, but I don't mind doing it if it's got to be done. (*Leans back in his chair*) You ought to take these things better, Oscar. I've made you money in the past. I'm going to make you more money now. You'll be a very rich man. What's the difference to any of us if a little more goes here, a little less goes there—it's all in the family. And it will stay in the family. I'll never marry. (ADDIE *enters, begins to gather the glasses from the table.* OSCAR *turns to* BEN) So my money will go to Alexandra and Leo. They may even marry some day and— (ADDIE *looks at* BEN.)

BIRDIE

(*Rising*)

Marry—Zan and Leo—

OSCAR

(*Carefully*)

That would make a great difference in my feelings. If they married.

BEN

Yes, that's what I mean. Of course it would make a difference.

OSCAR

(*Carefully*)

Is that what *you* mean, Regina?

REGINA

Oh, it's too far away. We'll talk about it in a few years.

OSCAR

I want to talk about it now.

BEN

(*Nods*)

Naturally.

REGINA

There's a lot of things to consider. They are first cousins, and—

OSCAR

That isn't unusual. Our grandmother and grandfather were first cousins.

REGINA

(*Giggles*)

And look at us.

(BEN *giggles.*)

OSCAR

(*Angrily*)

You're both being very gay with my money.

BEN

(*Sighs*)

These quarrels. I dislike them so. (*Leans forward to* REGINA) A marriage might be a very wise arrangement, for several reasons. And then, Oscar has given up something for you. You should try to manage something for him.

REGINA

I haven't said I was opposed to it. But Leo is a wild boy. There were those times when he took a little money from the bank and—

OSCAR

That's all past history—

REGINA

Oh, I know. And I know all young men are wild. I'm only mentioning it to show you that there are considerations—

BEN

(*Irritated because she does not understand that he is trying to keep* OSCAR *quiet*)

All right, so there are. But please assure Oscar that you will think about it very seriously.

REGINA

(*Smiles, nods*)

Very well. I assure Oscar that I will think about it seriously.

OSCAR

(*Sharply*)

That is not an answer.

REGINA

(*Rises*)

My, you're in a bad humor and you shall put me in one. I have said all that I am willing to say now. After all, Horace has to give his consent, too.

OSCAR

Horace will do what you tell him to.

REGINA

Yes, I think he will.

OSCAR

And I have your word that you will try to—

REGINA

(*Patiently*)

Yes, Oscar. You have my word that I will think about it. Now do leave me alone.

(*There is the sound of the front door being closed.*)

BIRDIE

I—Alexandra is only seventeen. She—

REGINA

(Calling)

Alexandra? Are you back?

ALEXANDRA

Yes, Mama.

LEO

(Comes into the room)

Mr. Marshall got off safe and sound. Weren't those fine clothes he had? You can always spot clothes made in a good place. Looks like maybe they were done in England. Lots of men in the North send all the way to England for their stuff.

BEN

(To LEO*)*

Were you careful driving the horses?

LEO

Oh, yes, sir. I was.

(ALEXANDRA *has come in on* BEN'S *question, hears the answer, looks angrily at* LEO.)

ALEXANDRA

It's a lovely night. You should have come, Aunt Birdie.

REGINA

Were you gracious to Mr. Marshall?

ALEXANDRA

I think so, Mama. I liked him.

REGINA

Good. And now I have great news for you. You are going to Baltimore in the morning to bring your father home.

ALEXANDRA

(*Gasps, then delighted*)

Me? Papa said I should come? That must mean— (*Turns to* ADDIE) Addie, he must be well. Think of it, he'll be back home again. We'll bring him home.

REGINA

You are going alone, Alexandra.

ADDIE

(ALEXANDRA *has turned in surprise*)

Going alone? Going by herself? A child that age! Mr. Horace ain't going to like Zan traipsing up there by herself.

REGINA

(*Sharply*)

Go upstairs and lay out Alexandra's things.

ADDIE

He'd expect me to be along—

REGINA

I'll be up in a few minutes to tell you what to pack. (ADDIE *slowly begins to climb the steps. To* ALEXANDRA) I should think you'd like going alone. At your age it certainly would have delighted me. You're a strange girl, Alexandra. Addie has babied you so much.

ALEXANDRA

I only thought it would be more fun if Addie and I went together.

BIRDIE

(*Timidly*)

Maybe I could go with her, Regina. I'd really like to.

REGINA

She is going alone. She is getting old enough to take some responsibilities.

OSCAR

She'd better learn now. She's almost old enough to get married. (*Jovially, to* LEO, *slapping him on shoulder*) Eh, son?

LEO

Huh?

OSCAR

(*Annoyed with* LEO *for not understanding*)

Old enough to get married, you're thinking, eh?

LEO

Oh, yes, sir. (*Feebly*) Lots of girls get married at Zan's age. Look at Mary Prester and Johanna and—

REGINA

Well, she's not getting married tomorrow. But she is going to Baltimore tomorrow, so let's talk about that. (*To* ALEXANDRA) You'll be glad to have Papa home again.

ALEXANDRA

I wanted to go before, Mama. You remember that. But you said *you* couldn't go, and that *I* couldn't go alone.

REGINA

I've changed my mind. (*Too casually*) You're to tell Papa how much you missed him, and that he must come home now —for your sake. Tell him that you *need* him home.

ALEXANDRA

Need him home? I don't understand.

REGINA

There is nothing for you to understand. You are simply to say what I have told you.

BIRDIE

(*Rises*)

He may be too sick. She couldn't do that—

ALEXANDRA

Yes. He may be too sick to travel. I couldn't make him think he had to come home for me, if he is too sick to—

REGINA

(*Looks at her, sharply, challengingly*)

You *couldn't* do what I tell you to do, Alexandra?

ALEXANDRA

(*Quietly*)

No. I couldn't. If I thought it would hurt him.

REGINA

(*After a second's silence, smiles pleasantly*)

But you are doing this for Papa's own good. (*Takes* ALEX-

ANDRA's *hand*) You must let me be the judge of his condition. It's the best possible cure for him to come home and be taken care of here. He mustn't stay there any longer and listen to those alarmist doctors. You are doing this entirely for his sake. Tell your papa that I want him to come home, that I miss him very much.

ALEXANDRA

(*Slowly*)

Yes, Mama.

REGINA

(*To the others. Rises*)

I must go and start getting Alexandra ready now. Why don't you all go home?

BEN

(*Rises*)

I'll attend to the railroad ticket. One of the boys will bring it over. Good night, everybody. Have a nice trip, Alexandra. The food on the train is very good. The celery is so crisp. Have a good time and act like a little lady. (*Exits*)

REGINA

Good night, Ben. Good night, Oscar— (*Playfully*) Don't be so glum, Oscar. It makes you look as if you had chronic indigestion.

BIRDIE

Good night, Regina.

REGINA

Good night, Birdie. (*Exits upstairs.*)

OSCAR

(*Starts for hall*)

Come along.

LEO

(*To* ALEXANDRA)

Imagine your not wanting to go! What a little fool you are. Wish it were me. What I could do in a place like Baltimore!

ALEXANDRA

(*Angrily, looking away from him*)

Mind your business. I can guess the kind of things *you* could do.

LEO

(*Laughs*)

Oh, no, you couldn't. (*He exits.*)

REGINA

(*Calling from the top of the stairs*)

Come on, Alexandra.

BIRDIE

(*Quickly, softly*)

Zan.

ALEXANDRA

I don't understand about my going, Aunt Birdie. (*Shrugs*) But anyway, Papa will be home again. (*Pats* BIRDIE's *arm*) Don't worry about me. I can take care of myself. Really I can.

BIRDIE

(*Shakes her head, softly*)

That's not what I'm worried about. Zan—

ALEXANDRA

(*Comes close to her*)

What's the matter?

BIRDIE

It's about Leo—

ALEXANDRA

(*Whispering*)

He beat the horses. That's why we were late getting back. We had to wait until they cooled off. He always beats the horses as if—

BIRDIE

(*Whispering frantically, holding* ALEXANDRA'S *hands*)

He's my son. My own son. But you are more to me—more to me than my own child. I love you more than anybody else—

ALEXANDRA

Don't worry about the horses. I'm sorry I told you.

BIRDIE

(*Her voice rising*)

I am not worrying about the horses. I am worrying about *you.* You are *not* going to marry Leo. I am not going to let them do that to you—

ALEXANDRA

Marry? To Leo? (*Laughs*) I wouldn't marry, Aunt Birdie. I've never even thought about it—

BIRDIE

But they have thought about it. (*Wildly*) Zan, I couldn't stand to think about such a thing. You and—

(OSCAR *has come into the doorway on* ALEXANDRA'S *speech. He is standing quietly, listening.*)

ALEXANDRA

(*Laughs*)

But I'm not going to marry. And I'm certainly not going to marry Leo.

BIRDIE

Don't you understand? They'll make you. They'll make you—

ALEXANDRA

(*Takes* BIRDIE'S *hands, quietly, firmly*)

That's foolish, Aunt Birdie. I'm grown now. Nobody can make me do anything.

BIRDIE

I just couldn't stand—

OSCAR

(*Sharply*)

Birdie. (BIRDIE *looks up, draws quickly away from* ALEXANDRA. *She stands rigid, frightened. Quietly*) Birdie, get your hat and coat.

ADDIE

(*Calls from upstairs*)

Come on, baby. Your mama's waiting for you, and she ain't nobody to keep waiting.

ALEXANDRA

All right. (*Then softly, embracing* BIRDIE) Good night, Aunt Birdie. (*As she passes* OSCAR) Good night, Uncle Oscar. (BIRDIE *begins to move slowly towards the door as* ALEXANDRA *climbs the stairs.* ALEXANDRA *is almost out of view when* BIRDIE *reaches* OSCAR *in the doorway. As* BIRDIE *quickly attempts to pass him, he slaps her hard, across the face.* BIRDIE *cries out, puts her hand to her face. On the cry,* ALEXANDRA *turns, begins to run down the stairs*) Aunt Birdie! What happened? What happened? I—

BIRDIE

(*Softly, without turning*)

Nothing, darling. Nothing happened. (*Quickly, as if anxious to keep* ALEXANDRA *from coming close*) Now go to bed. (OSCAR *exits*) Nothing happened. (*Turns to* ALEXANDRA *who is holding her hand*) I only—I only twisted my ankle. (*She goes out.* ALEXANDRA *stands on the stairs looking after her as if she were puzzled and frightened.*)

Curtain

Act Two

SCENE: *Same as Act One. A week later, morning.*

AT RISE: *The light comes from the open shutter of the right window; the other shutters are tightly closed.* ADDIE *is standing at the window, looking out. Near the dining-room doors are brooms, mops, rags, etc. After a second,* OSCAR *comes into the entrance hall, looks in the room, shivers, decides not to take his hat and coat off, comes into the room. At the sound of the door,* ADDIE *turns to see who has come in.*

ADDIE

(*Without interest*)

Oh, it's you, Mr. Oscar.

OSCAR

What is this? It's not night. What's the matter here? (*Shivers*) Fine thing at this time of the morning. Blinds all closed. (ADDIE *begins to open shutters.*) Where's Miss Regina? It's cold in here.

ADDIE

Miss Regina ain't down yet.

OSCAR

She had any word?

ADDIE

(*Wearily*)

No, sir.

OSCAR

Wouldn't you think a girl that age could get on a train at one place and have sense enough to get off at another?

ADDIE

Something must have happened. If Zan say she was coming last night, she's coming last night. Unless something happened. Sure fire disgrace to let a baby like that go all that way alone to bring home a sick man without—

OSCAR

You do a lot of judging around here, Addie, eh? Judging of your white folks, I mean.

ADDIE

(*Looks at him, sighs*)

I'm tired. I been up all night watching for them.

REGINA

(*Speaking from the upstairs hall*)

Who's downstairs, Addie? (*She appears in a dressing gown, peers down from the landing.* ADDIE *picks up broom, dustpan and brush and exits*) Oh, it's you, Oscar. What are you doing here so early? I haven't been down yet. I'm not finished dressing.

OSCAR

(*Speaking up to her*)

You had any word from them?

REGINA

No.

OSCAR

Then something certainly has happened. People don't just say they are arriving on Thursday night, and they haven't come by Friday morning.

REGINA

Oh, nothing has happened. Alexandra just hasn't got sense enough to send a message.

OSCAR

If nothing's happened, then why aren't they here?

REGINA

You asked me that ten times last night. My, you do fret so, Oscar. Anything might have happened. They may have missed connections in Atlanta, the train may have been delayed—oh, a hundred things could have kept them.

OSCAR

Where's Ben?

REGINA

(*As she disappears upstairs*)

Where should he be? At home, probably. Really, Oscar, I don't tuck him in his bed and I don't take him out of it. Have some coffee and don't worry so much.

OSCAR

Have some coffee? There isn't any coffee. (*Looks at his watch, shakes his head. After a second* CAL *enters with a large silver tray, coffee urn, small cups, newspaper*) Oh, there you are. Is everything in this fancy house always late?

CAL

(*Looks at him surprised*)

You ain't out shooting this morning, Mr. Oscar?

OSCAR

First day I missed since I had my head cold. First day I missed in eight years.

CAL

Yes, sir. I bet you. Simon he say you had a mighty good day yesterday morning. That's what Simon say. (*Brings* OSCAR *coffee and newspaper.*)

OSCAR

Pretty good, pretty good.

CAL

(*Laughs gayly*)

Bet you got enough bobwhite and squirrel to give every nigger in town a Jesus-party. Most of 'em ain't had no meat since the cotton picking was over. Bet they'd give anything for a little piece of that meat—

OSCAR

(*Turns his head to look at* CAL)

Cal, if I catch a nigger in this town going shooting, you know what's going to happen.

(LEO *enters.*)

CAL

(*Hastily*)

Yes, sir, Mr. Oscar. I didn't say nothing about nothing. It was Simon who told me and— Morning, Mr. Leo. You gentlemen having your breakfast with us here?

LEO

The boys in the bank don't know a thing. They haven't had any message.

(CAL *waits for an answer, gets none, shrugs, moves to door, exits.*)

OSCAR

(*Peers at* LEO)

What you doing here, son?

LEO

You told me to find out if the boys at the bank had any message from Uncle Horace or Zan—

OSCAR

I told you if they had a message to bring it here. I told you that if they didn't have a message to stay at the bank and do your work.

LEO

Oh, I guess I misunderstood.

OSCAR

You didn't misunderstand. You just were looking for any excuse to take an hour off. (LEO *pours a cup of coffee*) You got to stop that kind of thing. You got to start settling down. You going to be a married man one of these days.

LEO

Yes, sir.

OSCAR

You also got to stop with that woman in Mobile. (*As* LEO *is about to speak*) You're young and I haven't got no objections to outside women. That is, I haven't got no objections so long as they don't interfere with serious things. Outside women are all right in their place, but *now* isn't their place. You got to realize that.

LEO

(*Nods*)

Yes, sir. I'll tell her. She'll act all right about it.

OSCAR

Also, you got to start working harder at the bank. You got to convince your Uncle Horace you going to make a fit husband for Alexandra.

LEO

What do you think has happened to them? Supposed to be here last night— (*Laughs*) Bet you Uncle Ben's mighty worried. Seventy-five thousand dollars worried.

OSCAR

(*Smiles happily*)

Ought to be worried. Damn well ought to be. First he don't answer the letters, then he don't come home— (*Giggles.*)

LEO

What will happen if Uncle Horace don't come home or don't—

OSCAR

Or don't put up the money? Oh, we'll get it from outside. Easy enough.

LEO

(*Surprised*)

But *you* don't want outsiders.

OSCAR

What do I care who gets my share? I been shaved already. Serve Ben right if he had to give away some of his.

LEO

Damn shame what they did to you.

OSCAR

(*Looking up the stairs*)

Don't talk so loud. Don't you worry. When I die, you'll have as much as the rest. You might have yours *and* Alexandra's. I'm not so easily licked.

LEO

I wasn't thinking of myself, Papa—

OSCAR

Well, you should be, you should be. It's every man's duty to think of himself.

LEO

You think Uncle Horace don't want to go in on this?

OSCAR

(*Giggles*)

That's my hunch. He hasn't showed any signs of loving it yet.

LEO

(*Laughs*)

But he hasn't listened to Aunt Regina yet, either. Oh, he'll go along. It's too good a thing. Why wouldn't he want to? He's got plenty and plenty to invest with. He don't even have to sell anything. Eighty-eight thousand worth of Union Pacific bonds sitting right in his safe deposit box. All he's got to do is open the box.

OSCAR

(*After a pause. Looks at his watch*)

Mighty late breakfast in this fancy house. Yes, he's had those bonds for fifteen years. Bought them when they were low and just locked them up.

LEO

Yeah. Just has to open the box and take them out. That's all. Easy as easy can be. (*Laughs*) The things in that box! There's all those bonds, looking mighty fine. (OSCAR *slowly puts down his newspaper and turns to* LEO) Then right next to them is a baby shoe of Zan's and a cheap old cameo on a string, and, *and*—nobody'd believe this—a piece of an old violin. Not even a whole violin. Just a piece of an old thing, a piece of a violin.

OSCAR

(*Very softly, as if he were trying to control his voice*)

A piece of a violin! What do you think of that!

LEO

Yes, sirree. A lot of other crazy things, too. A poem, I guess it is, signed with his mother's name, and two old schoolbooks with notes and— (LEO *catches* OSCAR'S *look. His voice trails off. He turns his head away.*)

OSCAR

(*Very softly*)

How do you know what's in the box, son?

LEO

(*Stops, draws back, frightened, realizing what he has said*) Oh, well. Well, er. Well, one of the boys, sir. It was one of the boys at the bank. He took old Manders' keys. It was Joe Horns. He just up and took Manders' keys and, and—well, took the box out. (*Quickly*) Then they all asked me if I wanted to see, too. So I looked a little, I guess, but then I made them close up the box quick and I told them never—

OSCAR

(*Looks at him*)

Joe Horns, you say? He opened it?

LEO

Yes, sir, yes, he did. My word of honor. (*Very nervously looking away*) I suppose that don't excuse *me* for looking— (*Looking at* OSCAR) but I did make him close it up and put the keys back in Manders' drawer—

OSCAR

(*Leans forward, very softly*)

Tell me the truth, Leo. I am not going to be angry with you. Did you open the box yourself?

LEO

No, sir, I didn't. I told you I didn't. No, I—

OSCAR

(*Irritated, patient*)

I am *not* going to be angry with you. (*Watching* LEO *carefully*) Sometimes a young fellow deserves credit for looking round him to see what's going on. Sometimes that's a good sign in a fellow your age. (OSCAR *rises*) Many great men have made their fortune with their eyes. Did you open the box?

LEO

(*Very puzzled*)

No. I—

OSCAR

(*Moves to* LEO)

Did you open the box? It may have been—well, it may have been a good thing if you had.

LEO

(*After a long pause*)

I opened it.

OSCAR

(*Quickly*)

Is that the truth? (LEO *nods*) Does anybody else know that

you opened it? Come, Leo, don't be afraid of speaking the truth to me.

LEO

No. Nobody knew. Nobody was in the bank when I did it. But—

OSCAR

Did your Uncle Horace ever know you opened it?

LEO

(*Shakes his head*)

He only looks in it once every six months when he cuts the coupons, and sometimes Manders even does that for him. Uncle Horace don't even have the keys. Manders keeps them for him. Imagine not looking at all that. You can bet if I had the bonds, I'd watch 'em like—

OSCAR

If you had them. (LEO *watches him*) *If* you had them. Then you could have a share in the mill, you and me. A fine, big share, too. (*Pauses, shrugs*) Well, a man can't be shot for wanting to see his son get on in the world, can he, boy?

LEO

(*Looks up, begins to understand*)

No, he can't. Natural enough. (*Laughs*) But I haven't got the bonds and Uncle Horace has. And now he can just sit back and wait to be a millionaire.

OSCAR

(*Innocently*)

You think your Uncle Horace likes you well enough to lend you the bonds if he decides not to use them himself?

LEO

Papa, it must be that you haven't had your breakfast! (*Laughs loudly*) Lend me the bonds! My God—

OSCAR

(*Disappointed*)

No, I suppose not. Just a fancy of mine. A loan for three months, maybe four, easy enough for us to pay it back then. Anyway, this is only April— (*Slowly counting the months on his fingers*) and if he doesn't look at them until Fall, he wouldn't even miss them out of the box.

LEO

That's it. He wouldn't even miss them. Ah, well—

OSCAR

No, sir. Wouldn't even miss them. How could he miss them if he never looks at them? (*Sighs as* LEO *stares at him*) Well, here we are sitting around waiting for him to come home and invest his money in something he hasn't lifted his hand to get. But I can't help thinking he's acting strange. You laugh when I say he could lend you the bonds if he's not going to use them himself. But would it hurt him?

LEO

(*Slowly looking at* OSCAR)

No. No, it wouldn't.

OSCAR

People ought to help other people. But that's not always the way it happens. (BEN *enters, hangs his coat and hat in hall. Very carefully*) And so sometimes you got to think of yourself. (*As* LEO *stares at him,* BEN *appears in the doorway*) Morning, Ben.

BEN

(*Coming in, carrying his newspaper*)

Fine sunny morning. Any news from the runaways?

REGINA

(*On the staircase*)

There's no news or you would have heard it. Quite a convention so early in the morning, aren't you all? (*Goes to coffee urn.*)

OSCAR

You rising mighty late these days. Is that the way they do things in Chicago society?

BEN

(*Looking at his paper*)

Old Carter died up in Senateville. Eighty-one is a good time for us all, eh? What do you think has really happened to Horace, Regina?

REGINA

Nothing.

BEN

(*Too casually*)

You don't think maybe he never started from Baltimore and never intends to start?

REGINA

(*Irritated*)

Of course they've started. Didn't I have a letter from Alexandra? What is so strange about people arriving late? He has that cousin in Savannah he's so fond of. He may have stopped to see him. They'll be along today some time, very flattered that you and Oscar are so worried about them.

BEN

I'm a natural worrier. Especially when I am getting ready to close a business deal and one of my partners remains silent *and* invisible.

REGINA

(*Laughs*)

Oh, is that it? I thought you were worried about Horace's health.

OSCAR

Oh, that too. Who could help but worry? I'm worried. This is the first day I haven't shot since my head cold.

REGINA

(*Starts towards dining room*)

Then you haven't had your breakfast. Come along. (OSCAR *and* LEO *follow her.*)

BEN

Regina. (*She turns at dining-room door*) That cousin of Horace's has been dead for years and, in any case, the train does not go through Savannah.

REGINA

(*Laughs, continues into dining room, seats herself*)

Did he die? You're always remembering about people dying. (BEN *rises*) Now I intend to eat my breakfast in peace, and read my newspaper.

BEN

(*Goes towards dining room as he talks*)

This is second breakfast for me. My first was bad. Celia ain't the cook she used to be. Too old to have taste any more. If she hadn't belonged to Mama, I'd send her off to the country.

(OSCAR *and* LEO *start to eat.* BEN *seats himself.*)

LEO

Uncle Horace will have some tales to tell, I bet. Baltimore is a lively town.

REGINA

(*To* CAL)

The grits isn't hot enough. Take it back.

CAL

Oh, yes'm. (*Calling into kitchen as he exits*) Grits didn't hold the heat. Grits didn't hold the heat.

LEO

When I was at school three of the boys and myself took a train once and went over to Baltimore. It was so big we thought we were in Europe. I was just a kid then—

REGINA

I find it very pleasant (ADDIE *enters*) to have breakfast alone. I hate chattering before I've had something hot. (CAL *closes the dining-room doors*) Do be still, Leo.

(ADDIE *comes into the room, begins gathering up the cups, carries them to the large tray. Outside there are the sounds of voices. Quickly* ADDIE *runs into the hall. A few seconds later she appears again in the doorway, her arm around the shoulders of* HORACE GIDDENS, *supporting him.* HORACE *is a tall man of about forty-five. He has been good looking, but now his face is tired and ill. He walks stiffly, as if it were an enormous effort, and carefully, as if he were unsure of his balance.* ADDIE *takes off his overcoat and hangs it on the hall tree. She then helps him to a chair.*)

HORACE

How are you, Addie? How have you been?

ADDIE

I'm all right, Mr. Horace. I've just been worried about you.

(ALEXANDRA *enters. She is flushed and excited, her hat awry, her face dirty. Her arms are full of packages, but she comes quickly to* ADDIE.)

ALEXANDRA

Now don't tell me how worried you were. We couldn't help it and there was no way to send a message.

ADDIE

(*Begins to take packages from* ALEXANDRA)

Yes, sir, I was mighty worried.

ALEXANDRA

We had to stop in Mobile over night. Papa— (*Looks at him*) Papa didn't feel well. The trip was too much for him, and I made him stop and rest— (*As* ADDIE *takes the last package*) No, don't take that. That's father's medicine. I'll hold it. It mustn't break. Now, about the stuff outside. Papa must have his wheel chair. I'll get that and the valises—

ADDIE

(Very happy, holding ALEXANDRA'S *arms)*

Since when you got to carry your own valises? Since when I ain't old enough to hold a bottle of medicine? (HORACE *coughs)* You feel all right, Mr. Horace?

HORACE

(Nods)

Glad to be sitting down.

ALEXANDRA

(Opening package of medicine)

He doesn't feel all right. (ADDIE *looks at her, then at* HORACE) He just says that. The trip was very hard on him, and now he must go right to bed.

ADDIE

(Looking at him carefully)

Them fancy doctors, they give you help?

HORACE

They did their best.

ALEXANDRA

(Has become conscious of the voices in the dining room)

I bet Mama was worried. I better tell her we're here now. *(She starts for door.)*

HORACE

Zan. *(She stops)* Not for a minute, dear.

ALEXANDRA

Oh, Papa, you feel bad again. I knew you did. Do you want your medicine?

HORACE

No, I don't feel that way. I'm just tired, darling. Let me rest a little.

ALEXANDRA

Yes, but Mama will be mad if I don't tell her we're here.

ADDIE

They're all in there eating breakfast.

ALEXANDRA

Oh, are they all here? Why do they *always* have to be here? I was hoping Papa wouldn't have to see anybody, that it would be nice for him and quiet.

ADDIE

Then let your papa rest for a minute.

HORACE

Addie, I bet your coffee's as good as ever. They don't have such good coffee up North. (*Looks at the urn*) Is it as good, Addie? (ADDIE *starts for coffee urn.*)

ALEXANDRA

No. Dr. Reeves said not much coffee. Just now and then. I'm the nurse now, Addie.

ADDIE

You'd be a better one if you didn't look so dirty. Now go and take a bath, Miss Grown-up. Change your linens, get out a fresh dress and give your hair a good brushing—go on—

ALEXANDRA

Will you be all right, Papa?

ADDIE

Go on.

ALEXANDRA

(*On stairs, talks as she goes up*)

The pills Papa must take once every four hours. And the bottle only when—only if he feels very bad. Now don't move until I come back and don't talk much and remember about his medicine, Addie—

ADDIE

Ring for Belle and have her help you and then I'll make you a fresh breakfast.

ALEXANDRA

(*As she disappears*)

How's Aunt Birdie? Is she here?

ADDIE

It ain't right for you to have coffee? It will hurt you?

HORACE

(*Slowly*)

Nothing can make much difference now. Get me a cup, Addie. (*She looks at him, crosses to urn, pours a cup*) Funny. They can't make coffee up North. (ADDIE *brings him a cup*) They don't like red pepper, either. (*He takes the cup and gulps it greedily*) God, that's good. You remember how I used to drink it? Ten, twelve cups a day. So strong it had to stain the cup. (*Then slowly*) Addie, before I see anybody else, I want to know why Zan came to fetch me home. She's tried to tell me, but she doesn't seem to know herself.

ADDIE

(*Turns away*)

I don't know. All I know is big things are going on. Everybody going to be high-tone rich. Big rich. You too. All because smoke's going to start out of a building that ain't even up yet.

HORACE

I've heard about it.

ADDIE

And, er— (*Hesitates—steps to him*) And—well, Zan, she going to marry Mr. Leo in a little while.

HORACE

(*Looks at her, then very slowly*)

What are you talking about?

ADDIE

That's right. That's the talk, God help us.

HORACE

(*Angrily*)

What's the talk?

ADDIE

I'm telling you. There's going to be a wedding— (*Angrily turns away*) Over my dead body there is.

HORACE

(*After a second, quietly*)

Go and tell them I'm home.

ADDIE

(*Hesitates*)

Now you ain't to get excited. You're to be in your bed—

HORACE

Go on, Addie. Go and say I'm back. (ADDIE *opens dining-room doors. He rises with difficulty, stands stiff, as if he were in pain, facing the dining room.*)

ADDIE

Miss Regina. They're home. They got here—

REGINA

Horace! (REGINA *quickly rises, runs into the room. Warmly*) Horace! You've finally arrived. (*As she kisses him, the others come forward, all talking together.*)

BEN

(*In doorway, carrying a napkin*)

Well, sir, you had us all mighty worried. (*He steps forward. They shake hands.* ADDIE *exits.*)

OSCAR

You're a sight for sore eyes.

HORACE

Hello, Ben.

(LEO *enters, eating a biscuit.*)

OSCAR

And how you feel? Tip-top, I bet, because that's the way you're looking.

HORACE

(*Coldly, irritated with* OSCAR's *lie*)

Hello, Oscar. Hello, Leo, how are you?

LEO

(*Shaking hands*)

I'm fine, sir. But a lot better now that you're back.

REGINA

Now sit down. What did happen to you and where's Alexandra? I am so excited about seeing you that I almost forgot about her.

HORACE

I didn't feel good, a little weak, I guess, and we stopped over night to rest. Zan's upstairs washing off the train dirt.

REGINA

Oh, I am so sorry the trip was hard on you. I didn't think that—

HORACE

Well, it's just as if I had never been away. All of you here—

BEN

Waiting to welcome you home.

(BIRDIE *bursts in. She is wearing a flannel kimono and her face is flushed and excited.*)

BIRDIE

(*Runs to him, kisses him*)

Horace!

HORACE

(*Warmly pressing her arm*)

I was just wondering where you were, Birdie.

BIRDIE

(*Excited*)

Oh, I would have been here. I didn't know you were back until Simon said he saw the buggy. (*She draws back to look at him. Her face sobers*) Oh, you don't look well, Horace. No, you don't.

REGINA

(*Laughs*)

Birdie, what a thing to say—

HORACE

(*Looking at* OSCAR)

Oscar thinks I look very well.

OSCAR

(*Annoyed. Turns on* LEO)

Don't stand there holding that biscuit in your hand.

LEO

Oh, well. I'll just finish my breakfast, Uncle Horace, and then I'll give you all the news about the bank— (*He exits into the dining room.*)

OSCAR

And what is that costume you have on?

BIRDIE

(*Looking at* HORACE)

Now that you're home, you'll feel better. Plenty of good rest and we'll take such fine care of you. (*Stops*) But where is Zan? I missed her so much.

OSCAR

I asked you what is that strange costume you're parading around in?

BIRDIE

(*Nervously, backing towards stairs*)

Me? Oh! It's my wrapper. I was so excited about Horace I just rushed out of the house—

OSCAR

Did you come across the square dressed that way? My dear Birdie, I—

HORACE

(*To* REGINA, *wearily*)

Yes, it's just like old times.

REGINA

(*Quickly to* OSCAR)

Now, no fights. This is a holiday.

BIRDIE

(*Runs quickly up the stairs*)

Zan! Zannie!

OSCAR

Birdie! (*She stops.*)

BIRDIE

Oh. Tell Zan I'll be back in a little while. (*Whispers*) Sorry, Oscar. (*Exits.*)

REGINA

(*To* OSCAR *and* BEN)

Why don't you go finish your breakfast and let Horace rest for a minute?

BEN

(*Crossing to dining room with* OSCAR)

Never leave a meal unfinished. There are too many poor people who need the food. Mighty glad to see you home, Horace. Fine to have you back. Fine to have you back.

OSCAR

(*To* LEO *as* BEN *closes dining-room doors*)

Your mother has gone crazy. Running around the streets like a woman—

(*The moment* REGINA *and* HORACE *are alone, they become awkward and self-conscious.*)

REGINA

(*Laughs awkwardly*)

Well. Here we are. It's been a long time. (HORACE *smiles*) Five months. You know, Horace, I wanted to come and be with you in the hospital, but I didn't know where my duty was. Here, or with you. But you know how much I *wanted* to come.

HORACE

That's kind of you, Regina. There was no need to come.

REGINA

Oh, but there was. Five months lying there all by yourself, no kinfolks, no friends. Don't try to tell me you didn't have a bad time of it.

HORACE

I didn't have a bad time. (*As she shakes her head, he becomes insistent*) No, I didn't, Regina. Oh, at first when I—when I heard the news about myself—but after I got used to that, I liked it there.

REGINA

You *liked* it? (*Coldly*) Isn't that strange. You liked it so well you didn't want to come home?

HORACE

That's not the way to put it. (*Then, kindly, as he sees her turn her head away*) But there I was and I got kind of used to it, kind of to like lying there and thinking. (*Smiles*) I never had much time to think before. And time's become valuable to me.

REGINA

It sounds almost like a holiday.

HORACE

(*Laughs*)

It was, sort of. The first holiday I've had since I was a little kid.

REGINA

And here I was thinking you were in pain and—

HORACE

(*Quietly*)

I was in pain.

REGINA

And instead you were having a holiday! A holiday of thinking. Couldn't you have done that here?

HORACE

I wanted to do it before I came here. I was thinking about us.

REGINA

About us? About you and me? Thinking about you and me after all these years. (*Unpleasantly*) You shall tell me everything you thought—some day.

HORACE

(*There is silence for a minute*)

Regina. (*She turns to him*) Why did you send Zan to Baltimore?

REGINA

Why? Because I wanted you home. You can't make anything suspicious out of that, can you?

HORACE

I didn't mean to make anything suspicious about it. (*Hesitantly, taking her hand*) Zan said you wanted me to come home. I was so pleased at that and touched, it made me feel good.

REGINA

(*Taking away her hand, turns*)

Touched that I should want you home?

HORACE

(*Sighs*)

I'm saying all the wrong things as usual. Let's try to get along better. There isn't so much more time. Regina, what's all this crazy talk I've been hearing about Zan and Leo? Zan and Leo marrying?

REGINA

(*Turning to him, sharply*)

Who gossips so much around here?

HORACE

(*Shocked*)

Regina!

REGINA

(*Annoyed, anxious to quiet him*)

It's some foolishness that Oscar thought up. I'll explain later. I have no intention of allowing any such arrangement. It was simply a way of keeping Oscar quiet in all this business I've been writing you about—

HORACE

(*Carefully*)

What has Zan to do with any business of Oscar's? Whatever it is, you had better put it out of Oscar's head immediately. You know what I think of Leo.

REGINA

But there's no need to talk about it now.

HORACE

There is no need to talk about it ever. Not as long as I live.

(HORACE *stops, slowly turns to look at her*) As long as I live. I've been in a hospital for five months. Yet since I've been here you have not once asked me about—about my health. (*Then gently*) Well, I suppose they've written you. I can't live very long.

REGINA

(*Coldly*)

I've never understood why people have to talk about this kind of thing.

HORACE

(*There is a silence. Then he looks up at her, his face cold*)

You misunderstand. I don't intend to gossip about my sickness. I thought it was only fair to tell you. I was not asking for your sympathy.

REGINA

(*Sharply, turns to him*)

What do the doctors think caused your bad heart?

HORACE

What do you mean?

REGINA

They didn't think it possible, did they, that your fancy women may have—

HORACE

(*Smiles unpleasantly*)

Caused my heart to be bad? I don't think that's the best scientific theory. You don't catch heart trouble in bed.

REGINA

(*Angrily*)

I didn't think you did. I only thought you might catch a bad conscience—in bed, as you say.

HORACE

I didn't tell them about my bad conscience. Or about my fancy women. Nor did I tell them that my wife has not wanted me in bed with her for— (*Sharply*) How long is it, Regina? (REGINA *turns to him*) Ten years? Did you bring me home for this, to make me feel guilty again? That means you want something. But you'll not make me feel guilty any more. My "thinking" has made a difference.

REGINA

I see that it has. (*She looks towards dining-room door. Then comes to him, her manner warm and friendly*) It's foolish for us to fight this way. I didn't mean to be unpleasant. I was stupid.

HORACE

(*Wearily*)

God knows I didn't either. I came home wanting so much not to fight, and then all of a sudden there we were. I got hurt and—

REGINA

(*Hastily*)

It's all my fault. I didn't ask about—about your illness because I didn't want to remind you of it. Anyway I never believe doctors when they talk about— (*Brightly*) when they talk like that.

HORACE

(*Not looking at her*)

Well, we'll try our best with each other. (*He rises.*)

REGINA

(*Quickly*)

I'll try. Honestly, I will. Horace, Horace, I know you're

tired but, but—couldn't you stay down here a few minutes longer? I want Ben to tell you something.

HORACE

Tomorrow.

REGINA

I'd like to now. It's very important to me. It's very important to all of us. (*Gaily, as she moves toward dining room*) Important to your beloved daughter. She'll be a very great heiress—

HORACE

Will she? That's nice.

REGINA

(*Opens doors*)

Ben, are you finished breakfast?

HORACE

Is this the mill business I've had so many letters about?

REGINA

(*To* BEN)

Horace would like to talk to you now.

HORACE

Horace would not like to talk to you now. I am very tired, Regina—

REGINA

(*Comes to him*)

Please. You've said we'll try our best with each other. I'll try. Really, I will. Please do this for me now. You will see what I've done while you've been away. How I watched your interests. (*Laughs gaily*) And I've done very well too. But things can't be delayed any longer. Everything must be settled this week— (HORACE *sits down.* BEN *enters.* OSCAR *has stayed in the dining room, his head turned to watch them.* LEO *is pretending to read the newspaper*) Now you must tell Horace all about it. Only be quick because he is very tired and must go to bed. (HORACE *is looking up at her. His face hardens as she speaks*) But I think your news will be better for him than all the medicine in the world.

BEN

(*Looking at* HORACE)

It could wait. Horace may not feel like talking today.

REGINA

What an old faker you are! You know it can't wait. You know it must be finished this week. You've been just as anxious for Horace to get here as I've been.

BEN

(*Very jovial*)

I suppose I have been. And why not? Horace has done Hubbard Sons many a good turn. Why shouldn't I be anxious to help him now?

REGINA

(*Laughs*)

Help him! Help him when you need him, that's what you mean.

BEN

What a woman you married, Horace. (*Laughs awkwardly*

when HORACE *does not answer*) Well, then I'll make it quick. You know what I've been telling you for years. How I've always said that every one of us little Southern business men had great things—(*Extends his arm*)—right beyond our finger tips. It's been my dream: my dream to make those fingers grow longer. I'm a lucky man, Horace, a lucky man. To dream and to live to get what you've dreamed of. That's *my* idea of a lucky man. (*Looks at his fingers as his arm drops slowly*) For thirty years I've cried bring the cotton mills to the cotton. (HORACE *opens medicine bottle*) Well, finally I got up nerve to go to Marshall Company in Chicago.

HORACE

I know all this. (*He takes the medicine.* REGINA *rises, steps to him.*)

BEN

Can I get you something?

HORACE

Some water, please.

REGINA

(*Turns quickly*)

Oh, I'm sorry. Let me. (*Brings him a glass of water. He drinks as they wait in silence*) You feel all right now?

HORACE

Yes. You wrote me. I know all that.

(OSCAR *enters from dining room.*)

REGINA

(*Triumphantly*)

But you don't know that in the last few days Ben has agreed to give us—you, I mean—a much larger share.

HORACE

Really? That's very generous of him.

BEN

(*Laughs*)

It wasn't so generous of me. It was smart of Regina.

REGINA

(*As if she were signaling* HORACE)

I explained to Ben that perhaps you hadn't answered his letters because you didn't think he was offering you enough, and that the time was getting short and you could guess how much he needed you—

HORACE

(*Smiles at her, nods*)

And I could guess that he wants to keep control in the family?

REGINA

(*To* BEN, *triumphantly*)

Exactly. (*To* HORACE) So I did a little bargaining for you and convinced my brothers they weren't the only Hubbards who had a business sense.

HORACE

Did you have to convince them of that? How little people

know about each other! (*Laughs*) But you'll know better about Regina next time, eh, Ben? (BEN, REGINA, HORACE *laugh together.* OSCAR's *face is angry*) Now let's see. We're getting a bigger share. (*Looking at* OSCAR) Who's getting less?

BEN

Oscar.

HORACE

Well, Oscar, you've grown very unselfish. What's happened to you?

(LEO *enters from dining room.*)

BEN

(*Quickly, before* OSCAR *can answer*)

Oscar doesn't mind. Not worth fighting about now, eh, Oscar?

OSCAR

(*Angrily*)

I'll get mine in the end. You can be sure of that. I've got my son's future to think about.

HORACE

(*Sharply*)

Leo? Oh, I see. (*Puts his head back, laughs.* REGINA *looks at him nervously*) I am beginning to see. Everybody will get theirs.

BEN

I knew you'd see it. Seventy-five thousand, and that seventy-five thousand will make you a million.

REGINA

(*Steps to table, leaning forward*)

It will, Horace, it will.

HORACE

I believe you. (*After a second*) Now I can understand Oscar's self-sacrifice, but what did you have to promise Marshall Company besides the money you're putting up?

BEN

They wouldn't take promises. They wanted guarantees.

HORACE

Of what?

BEN

(*Nods*)

Water power. Free and plenty of it.

HORACE

You got them that, of course.

BEN

Cheap. You'd think the Governor of a great state would make his price a little higher. From pride, you know. (HORACE *smiles.* BEN *smiles*) Cheap wages. "What do you mean by cheap wages?" I say to Marshall. "Less than Massachusetts," he says to me, "and that averages eight a week." "Eight a week! By God," I tell him, "*I'd* work for eight a week myself." Why, there ain't a mountain white or a town nigger but wouldn't give his right arm for three silver dollars every week, eh, Horace?

HORACE

Sure. And they'll take less than that when you get around to playing them off against each other. You can save a little money that way, Ben. (*Angrily*) And make them hate each other just a little more than they do now.

REGINA

What's all this about?

BEN

(*Laughs*)

There'll be no trouble from anybody, white or black. Marshall said that to me. "What about strikes? That's all we've had in Massachusetts for the last three years." I say to him, "What's a strike? I never heard of one. Come South, Marshall. We got good folks and we don't stand for any fancy fooling."

HORACE

You're right. (*Slowly*) Well, it looks like you made a good deal for yourselves, and for Marshall, too. (*To* BEN) Your father used to say he made the thousands and you boys would make the millions. I think he was right. (*Rises.*)

REGINA

(*They are all looking at* HORACE. *She laughs nervously*)

Millions for *us,* too.

HORACE

Us? You and me? I don't think so. We've got enough money, Regina. We'll just sit by and watch the boys grow rich. (*They watch* HORACE *tensely as he begins to move towards the staircase. He passes* LEO, *looks at him for a second*) How's everything at the bank, Leo?

LEO

Fine, sir. Everything is fine.

HORACE

How are all the ladies in Mobile? (HORACE *turns to* REGINA, *sharply*) Whatever made you think I'd let Zan marry—

REGINA

Do you mean that you are turning this down? Is it possible that's what you mean?

BEN

No, that's not what he means. Turning down a fortune. Horace is tired. He'd rather talk about it tomorrow—

REGINA

We can't keep putting it off this way. Oscar must be in Chicago by the end of the week with the money and contracts.

OSCAR

(*Giggles, pleased*)

Yes, sir. Got to be there end of the week. No sense going without the money.

REGINA

(*Tensely*)

I've waited long enough for your answer. I'm not going to wait any longer.

HORACE

(*Very deliberately*)

I'm very tired now, Regina.

BEN

(*Hastily*)

Now, Horace probably has his reasons. Things he'd like explained. Tomorrow will do. I can—

REGINA

(*Turns to* BEN, *sharply*)

I want to know his reasons now! (*Turns back to* HORACE.)

HORACE

(*As he climbs the steps*)

I don't know them all myself. Let's leave it at that.

REGINA

We shall not leave it at that! We have waited for you here like children. Waited for you to come home.

HORACE

So that you could invest my money. So this is why you wanted me home? Well, I had hoped— (*Quietly*) If you are disappointed, Regina, I'm sorry. But I must do what I think best. We'll talk about it another day.

REGINA

We'll talk about it now. Just you and me.

HORACE

(*Looks down at her. His voice is tense*)

Please, Regina. It's been a hard trip. I don't feel well. Please leave me alone now.

REGINA

(*Quietly*)

I want to talk to you, Horace. I'm coming up. (*He looks at her for a minute, then moves on again out of sight. She begins to climb the stairs.*)

BEN

(*Softly.* REGINA *turns to him as he speaks*)

Sometimes it is better to wait for the sun to rise again. (*She does not answer*) And sometimes, as our mother used to tell you, (REGINA *starts up stairs*) it's unwise for a good-looking woman to frown. (BEN *rises, moves towards stairs*) Softness and a smile do more to the heart of men— (*She disappears.* BEN *stands looking up the stairs. There is a long silence. Then, suddenly,* OSCAR *giggles.*)

OSCAR

Let us hope she'll change his mind. Let us hope. (*After a second* BEN *crosses to table, picks up his newspaper.* OSCAR *looks at* BEN. *The silence makes* LEO *uncomfortable.*)

LEO

The paper says twenty-seven cases of yellow fever in New Orleans. Guess the flood-waters caused it. (*Nobody pays attention*) Thought they were building the levees high enough. Like the niggers always say: a man born of woman can't build nothing high enough for the Mississippi. (*Gets no answer. Gives an embarrassed laugh.*)

(*Upstairs there is the sound of voices. The voices are not loud, but* BEN, OSCAR, LEO *become conscious of them.* LEO *crosses to landing, looks up, listens.*)

OSCAR

(*Pointing up*)

Now just suppose she don't change his mind? Just suppose he keeps on refusing?

BEN

(*Without conviction*)

He's tired. It was a mistake to talk to him today. He's a sick man, but he isn't a crazy one.

OSCAR

(*Giggles*)

But just suppose he is crazy. What then?

BEN

(*Puts down his paper, peers at* OSCAR)

Then we'll go outside for the money. There's plenty who would give it.

OSCAR

And plenty who will want a lot for what they give. The ones who are rich enough to give will be smart enough to want. That means we'd be working for them, don't it, Ben?

BEN

You don't have to tell me the things I told you six months ago.

OSCAR

Oh, you're right not to worry. She'll change his mind. She always has. (*There is a silence. Suddenly* REGINA's *voice becomes louder and sharper. All of them begin to listen now. Slowly* BEN *rises, goes to listen by the staircase.* OSCAR, *watching him, smiles. As they listen* REGINA's *voice becomes very loud.* HORACE's *voice is no longer heard*) Maybe. But I don't believe it. I never did believe he was going in with us.

BEN

(*Turning on him*)

What the hell do you expect me to do?

OSCAR

(*Mildly*)

Nothing. You done your almighty best. Nobody could blame you if the whole thing just dripped away right through our fingers. You can't do a thing. But there may be something I could do for us. (OSCAR *rises*) Or, I might better say, Leo could do for us. (BEN *stops, turns, looks at* OSCAR. LEO *is staring at* OSCAR) Ain't that true, son? Ain't it true you might be able to help your own kinfolks?

LEO

(*Nervously taking a step to him*)

Papa, I—

BEN

(*Slowly*)

How would he help us, Oscar?

OSCAR

Leo's got a friend. Leo's friend owns eighty-eight thousand dollars in Union Pacific bonds. (BEN *turns to look at* LEO) Leo's friend don't look at the bonds much—not for five or six months at a time.

BEN

(*After a pause*)

Union Pacific. Uh, huh. Let me understand. Leo's friend would—would lend him these bonds and he—

OSCAR

(*Nods*)

Would be kind enough to lend them to us.

BEN

Leo.

LEO

(*Excited, comes to him*)

Yes, sir?

BEN

When would your friend be wanting the bonds back?

LEO

(*Very nervous*)

I don't know. I—well, I—

OSCAR

(*Sharply. Steps to him*)

You told me he won't look at them until Fall—

LEO

Oh, that's right. But I—not till Fall. Uncle Horace never—

BEN

(*Sharply*)

Be still.

OSCAR

(*Smiles at* LEO)

Your uncle doesn't wish to know your friend's name.

LEO

(*Starts to laugh*)

That's a good one. Not know his name—

OSCAR

Shut up, Leo! (LEO *turns away slowly, moves to table.* BEN *turns to* OSCAR) He won't look at them again until September. That gives us five months. Leo will return the bonds in three months. And we'll have no trouble raising the money once the mills are going up. Will Marshall accept bonds?

(BEN *stops to listen to sudden sharp voices from above. The voices are now very angry and very loud.*)

BEN

(*Smiling*)

Why not? Why not? (*Laughs*) Good. We are lucky. We'll take the loan from Leo's friend—I think he will make a safer partner than our sister. (*Nods towards stairs. Turns to* LEO) How soon can you get them?

LEO

Today. Right now. They're in the safe-deposit box and—

BEN

(*Sharply*)

I don't want to know where they are.

OSCAR

(*Laughs*)

We will keep it secret from you. (*Pats* BEN'S *arm.*)

BEN

(*Smiles*)

Good. Draw a check for our part. You can take the night train for Chicago. Well, Oscar (*holds out his hand*), good luck to us.

OSCAR

Leo will be taken care of?

LEO

I'm entitled to Uncle Horace's share. I'd enjoy being a partner—

BEN

(*Turns to stare at him*)

You would? You can go to hell, you little— (*Starts towards* LEO.)

OSCAR

(*Nervously*)

Now, now. He didn't mean that. I only want to be sure he'll get something out of all this.

BEN

Of course. We'll take care of him. We won't have any trouble about that. I'll see you at the store.

OSCAR

(*Nods*)

That's settled then. Come on, son. (*Starts for door.*)

LEO

(*Puts out his hand*)

I didn't mean just that. I was only going to say what a great day this was for me and— (BEN *ignores his hand.*)

BEN

Go on.

(LEO *looks at him, turns, follows* OSCAR *out.* BEN *stands where he is, thinking. Again the voices upstairs can be heard.* REGINA'S *voice is high and furious.* BEN *looks up, smiles, winces at the noise.*)

ALEXANDRA

(*Upstairs*)

Mama—Mama—don't . . . (*The noise of running footsteps is heard and* ALEXANDRA *comes running down the steps, speaking as she comes*) Uncle Ben! Uncle Ben! Please go up. Please make Mama stop. Uncle Ben, he's sick, he's so sick. How can Mama talk to him like that—please, make her stop. She'll—

BEN

Alexandra, you have a tender heart.

ALEXANDRA

(*Crying*)

Go on up, Uncle Ben, please—

(*Suddenly the voices stop. A second later there is the sound of a door being slammed.*)

BEN

Now you see. Everything is over. Don't worry. (*He starts for the door*) Alexandra, I want you to tell your mother how sorry I am that I had to leave. And don't worry so, my dear. Married folk frequently raise their voices, unfortunately. (*He starts to put on his hat and coat as* REGINA *appears on the stairs.*)

ALEXANDRA

(*Furiously*)

How can you treat Papa like this? He's sick. He's very sick. Don't you know that? I won't let you.

REGINA

Mind your business, Alexandra. (*To* BEN. *Her voice is cold and calm*) How much longer can you wait for the money?

BEN

(*Putting on his coat*)

He has refused? My, that's too bad.

REGINA

He will change his mind. I'll find a way to make him. What's the longest you can wait now?

BEN

I could wait until next week. But I can't wait until next

week. (*He giggles, pleased at the joke*) I could but I can't. Could and can't. Well, I must go now. I'm very late—

REGINA

(*Coming downstairs towards him*)

You're not going. I want to talk to you.

BEN

I was about to give Alexandra a message for you. I wanted to tell you that Oscar is going to Chicago tonight, so we can't be here for our usual Friday supper.

REGINA

(*Tensely*)

Oscar is going to Chi— (*Softly*) What do you mean?

BEN

Just that. Everything is settled. He's going on to deliver to Marshall—

REGINA

(*Taking a step to him*)

I demand to know what— You are lying. You are trying to scare me. *You haven't got the money.* How could you have it? You can't have— (BEN *laughs*) You will wait until I—

(HORACE *comes into view on the landing.*)

BEN

You are getting out of hand. Since when do I take orders from you?

REGINA

Wait, you— (BEN *stops*) How *can* he go to Chicago? Did

a ghost arrive with the money? (BEN *starts for the hall*) I don't believe you. Come back here. (REGINA *starts after him*) Come back here, you— (*The door slams. She stops in the doorway, staring, her fists clenched. After a pause she turns slowly.*)

HORACE

(*Very quietly*)

It's a great day when you and Ben cross swords. I've been waiting for it for years.

ALEXANDRA

Papa, Papa, please go back! You will—

HORACE

And so they don't need you, and so you will not have your millions, after all.

REGINA

(*Turns slowly*)

You hate to see anybody live now, don't you? You hate to think that I'm going to be alive and have what I want.

HORACE

I should have known you'd think that was the reason.

REGINA

Because you're going to die and you know you're going to die.

ALEXANDRA

(*Shrilly*)

Mama! Don't— Don't listen, Papa. Just don't listen. Go away—

HORACE

Not to keep you from getting what you want. Not even partly that. (*Holding to the rail*) I'm sick of you, sick of this house, sick of my life here. I'm sick of your brothers and their dirty tricks to make a dime. There must be better ways of getting rich than cheating niggers on a pound of bacon. Why should I give you the money? (*Very angrily*) To pound the bones of this town to make dividends for you to spend? You wreck the town, you and your brothers, *you* wreck the town and live on it. Not me. Maybe it's easy for the dying to be honest. But it's not my fault I'm dying. (ADDIE *enters, stands at door quietly*) I'll do no more harm now. I've done enough. I'll die my own way. And I'll do it without making the world any worse. I leave that to you.

REGINA

(*Looks up at him slowly, calmly*)

I hope you die. I hope you die soon. (*Smiles*) I'll be waiting for you to die.

ALEXANDRA

(*Shrieking*)

Papa! Don't— Don't listen— Don't—

ADDIE

Come here, Zan. Come out of this room.

(ALEXANDRA *runs quickly to* ADDIE, *who holds her.* HORACE *turns slowly and starts upstairs.*)

Curtain

Act Three

SCENE: *Same as Act One. Two weeks later. It is late afternoon and it is raining.*

AT RISE: HORACE *is sitting near the window in a wheel chair. On the table next to him is a safe-deposit box, and a small bottle of medicine.* BIRDIE *and* ALEXANDRA *are playing the piano. On a chair is a large sewing basket.*

BIRDIE

(*Counting for* ALEXANDRA)

One and two and three and four. One and two and three and four. (*Nods—turns to* HORACE) We once played together, Horace. Remember?

HORACE

(*Has been looking out of the window*)

What, Birdie?

BIRDIE

We played together. You and me.

ALEXANDRA

Papa used to play?

BIRDIE

Indeed he did. (ADDIE *appears at the door in a large kitchen apron. She is wiping her hands on a towel*) He played the fiddle and very well, too.

ALEXANDRA

(*Turns to smile at* HORACE)

I never knew—

ADDIE

Where's your mama?

ALEXANDRA

Gone to Miss Safronia's to fit her dresses.

(ADDIE *nods, starts to exit.*)

HORACE

Addie.

ADDIE

Yes, Mr. Horace.

HORACE

(*Speaks as if he had made a sudden decision*)

Tell Cal to get on his things. I want him to go an errand.

(ADDIE *nods, exits.* HORACE *moves nervously in his chair, looks out of the window.*)

ALEXANDRA

(*Who has been watching him*)

It's too bad it's been raining all day, Papa. But you can go out in the yard tomorrow. Don't be restless.

HORACE

I'm not restless, darling.

BIRDIE

I remember so well the time we played together, your papa and me. It was the first time Oscar brought me here to supper. I had never seen all the Hubbards together before, and you know what a ninny I am and how shy. (*Turns to look at* HORACE) You said you could play the fiddle and you'd be much obliged if I'd play with you. *I* was obliged to *you,* all right, all right. (*Laughs when he does not answer her*) Horace, you haven't heard a word I've said.

HORACE

Birdie, when did Oscar get back from Chicago?

BIRDIE

Yesterday. Hasn't he been here yet?

ALEXANDRA

(*Stops playing*)

No. Neither has Uncle Ben since—since that day.

BIRDIE

Oh, I didn't know it was *that* bad. Oscar never tells me anything—

HORACE

(*Smiles, nods*)

The Hubbards have had their great quarrel. I knew it would come some day. (*Laughs*) It came.

ALEXANDRA

It came. It certainly came all right.

BIRDIE

(*Amazed*)

But Oscar was in such a good humor when he got home, I didn't—

HORACE

Yes, I can understand that.

(ADDIE *enters carrying a large tray with glasses, a carafe of elderberry wine and a plate of cookies, which she puts on the table.*)

ALEXANDRA

Addie! A party! What for?

ADDIE

Nothing for. I had the fresh butter, so I made the cakes, and a little elderberry does the stomach good in the rain.

BIRDIE

Isn't this nice! A party just for us. Let's play party music, Zan.

(ALEXANDRA *begins to play a gay piece.*)

ADDIE

(*To* HORACE, *wheeling his chair to center*)

Come over here, Mr. Horace, and don't be thinking so much. A glass of elderberry will do more good.

(ALEXANDRA *reaches for a cake.* BIRDIE *pours herself a glass of wine.*)

ALEXANDRA

Good cakes, Addie. It's nice here. Just us. Be nice if it could always be this way.

BIRDIE

(*Nods happily*)

Quiet and restful.

ADDIE

Well, it won't be that way long. Little while now, even sitting here, you'll hear the red bricks going into place. The next day the smoke'll be pushing out the chimneys and by church time that Sunday every human born of woman will be living on chicken. That's how Mr. Ben's been telling the story.

HORACE

(*Looks at her*)

They believe it that way?

ADDIE

Believe it? They use to believing what Mr. Ben orders. There ain't been so much talk around here since Sherman's army didn't come near.

HORACE

(*Softly*)

They are fools.

ADDIE

(*Nods, sits down with the sewing basket*)

You ain't born in the South unless you're a fool.

BIRDIE

(*Has drunk another glass of wine*)

But we didn't play together after that night. Oscar said he didn't like me to play on the piano. (*Turns to* ALEXANDRA) You know what he said that night?

ALEXANDRA

Who?

BIRDIE

Oscar. He said that music made him nervous. He said he just sat and waited for the next note. (ALEXANDRA *laughs*) He wasn't poking fun. He meant it. Ah, well— (*She finishes her glass, shakes her head.* HORACE *looks at her, smiles*) Your papa don't like to admit it, but he's been mighty kind to me all these years. (*Running the back of her hand along his sleeve*) Often he'd step in when somebody said something and once— (*She stops, turns away, her face still*) Once he stopped Oscar from— (*She stops, turns. Quickly*) I'm sorry I said that. Why, here I am so happy and yet I think about bad things. (*Laughs nervously*) That's not right, now, is it? (*She pours a drink.* CAL *appears in the door. He has on an old coat and is carrying a torn umbrella.*)

ALEXANDRA

Have a cake, Cal.

CAL

(*Comes in, takes a cake*)

Yes'm. You want me, Mr. Horace?

HORACE

What time is it, Cal?

CAL

'Bout ten minutes before it's five.

HORACE

All right. Now you walk yourself down to the bank.

CAL

It'll be closed. Nobody'll be there but Mr. Manders, Mr. Joe Horns, Mr. Leo—

HORACE

Go in the back way. They'll be at the table, going over the day's business. (*Points to the deposit box*) See that box?

CAL

(*Nods*)

Yes, sir.

HORACE

You tell Mr. Manders that Mr. Horace says he's much obliged to him for bringing the box, it arrived all right.

CAL

(*Bewildered*)

He know you got the box. He bring it himself Wednesday. I opened the door to him and he say, "Hello, Cal, coming on to summer weather."

HORACE

You say just what I tell you. Understand?

(BIRDIE *pours another drink, stands at table.*)

CAL

No, sir. I ain't going to say I understand. I'm going down and tell a man he give you something he already know he give you, and you say "understand."

HORACE

Now, Cal.

CAL

Yes, sir. I just going to say you obliged for the box coming all right. I ain't going to understand it, but I'm going to say it.

HORACE

And tell him I want him to come over here after supper, and to bring Mr. Sol Fowler with him.

CAL

(*Nods*)

He's to come after supper and bring Mr. Sol Fowler, your attorney-*at*-law, with him.

HORACE

(*Smiles*)

That's right. Just walk right in the back room and say your piece. (*Slowly*) In front of everybody.

CAL

Yes, sir. (*Mumbles to himself as he exits.*)

ALEXANDRA

(*Who has been watching* HORACE)

Is anything the matter, Papa?

HORACE

Oh, no. Nothing.

ADDIE

Miss Birdie, that elderberry going to give you a headache spell.

BIRDIE

(*Beginning to be drunk. Gaily*)

Oh, I don't think so. I don't think it will.

ALEXANDRA

(*As* HORACE *puts his hand to his throat*)

Do you want your medicine, Papa?

HORACE

No, no. I'm all right, darling.

BIRDIE

Mama used to give me elderberry wine when I was a little girl. For hiccoughs. (*Laughs*) You know, I don't think people get hiccoughs any more. Isn't that funny? (BIRDIE *laughs.* HORACE *and* ALEXANDRA *laugh*) I used to get hiccoughs just when I shouldn't have.

ADDIE

(*Nods*)

And nobody gets growing pains no more. That is funny. Just as if there was some style in what you get. One year an ailment's stylish and the next year it ain't.

BIRDIE

(*Turns*)

I remember. It was my first big party, at Lionnet I mean, and I was so excited, and there I was with hiccoughs and Mama laughing. (*Softly. Looking at carafe*) Mama always laughed. (*Picks up carafe*) A big party, a lovely dress from Mr. Worth in Paris, France, and hiccoughs. (*Pours drink*) My brother pounding me on the back and Mama with the elderberry bottle, laughing at me. Everybody was on their way to come, and I was such a ninny, hiccoughing away. (*Drinks*) You know, that was the first day I ever saw Oscar Hubbard.

The Ballongs were selling their horses and he was going there to buy. He passed and lifted his hat—we could see him from the window—and my brother, to tease Mama, said maybe we should have invited the Hubbards to the party. He said Mama didn't like them because they kept a store, and he said that was old-fashioned of her. (*Her face lights up*) And then, and *then,* I saw Mama angry for the first time in my life. She said that wasn't the reason. She said she was old-fashioned, but not that way. She said she was old-fashioned enough not to like people who killed animals they couldn't use, and who made their money charging awful interest to poor, ignorant niggers and cheating them on what they bought. She was very angry, Mama was. I had never seen her face like that. And then suddenly she laughed and said, "Look, I've frightened Birdie out of the hiccoughs." (*Her head drops. Then softly*) And so she had. They were all gone. (*Moves to sofa, sits.*)

ADDIE

Yeah, they got mighty well off cheating niggers. Well, there are people who eat the earth and eat all the people on it like in the Bible with the locusts. Then there are people who stand around and watch them eat it. (*Softly*) Sometimes I think it ain't right to stand and watch them do it.

BIRDIE

(*Thoughtfully*)

Like I say, if we could only go back to Lionnet. Everybody'd be better there. They'd be good and kind. I like people to be kind. (*Pours drink*) Don't you, Horace; don't you like people to be kind?

HORACE

Yes, Birdie.

BIRDIE

(*Very drunk now*)

Yes, that was the first day I ever saw Oscar. Who would have thought— (*Quickly*) You all want to know something? Well, I don't like Leo. My very own son, and I don't like him. (*Laughs, gaily*) My, I guess I even like Oscar more.

ALEXANDRA

Why did you marry Uncle Oscar?

ADDIE

(*Sharply*)

That's no question for you to be asking.

HORACE

(*Sharply*)

Why not? She's heard enough around here to ask anything.

ALEXANDRA

Aunt Birdie, why did you marry Uncle Oscar?

BIRDIE

I don't know. I thought I liked him. He was kind to me and I thought it was because he liked me too. But that wasn't the reason— (*Wheels on* ALEXANDRA) Ask why *he* married *me*. I can tell you that: He's told it to me often enough.

ADDIE

(*Leaning forward*)

Miss Birdie, don't—

BIRDIE

(*Speaking very rapidly, tensely*)

My family was good and the cotton on Lionnet's fields was better. Ben Hubbard wanted the cotton and (*Rises*) Oscar Hubbard married it for him. He was kind to me, then. He used to smile at me. He hasn't smiled at me since. Everybody knew that's what he married me for. (ADDIE *rises*) Everybody but me. Stupid, stupid me.

ALEXANDRA

(*To* HORACE, *holding his hand, softly*)

I see. (*Hesitates*) Papa, I mean—when you feel better couldn't we go away? I mean, by ourselves. Couldn't we find a way to go—

HORACE

Yes, I know what you mean. We'll try to find a way. I promise you, darling.

ADDIE

(*Moves to* BIRDIE)

Rest a bit, Miss Birdie. You get talking like this you'll get a headache and—

BIRDIE

(*Sharply, turning to her*)

I've never had a headache in my life. (*Begins to cry hysterically*) You know it as well as I do. (*Turns to* ALEXANDRA) I never had a headache, Zan. That's a lie they tell for me. I drink. All by myself, in my own room, by myself, I drink. Then, when they want to hide it, they say, "Birdie's got a headache again"—

ALEXANDRA

(*Comes to her quickly*)

Aunt Birdie.

BIRDIE

(*Turning away*)

Even you won't like me now. You won't like me any more.

ALEXANDRA

I love you. I'll always love you.

BIRDIE

(*Furiously*)

Well, don't. Don't love me. Because in twenty years you'll just be like me. They'll do all the same things to you. (*Begins to laugh hysterically*) You know what? In twenty-two years I haven't had a whole day of happiness. Oh, a little, like today with you all. But never a single, whole day. I say to myself, if only I had one more *whole* day, then— (*The laugh stops*) And that's the way you'll be. And you'll trail after them, just like me, hoping they won't be so mean that day or say something to make you feel so bad—only you'll be worse off because you haven't got my Mama to remember— (*Turns away, her head drops. She stands quietly, swaying a little, holding onto the sofa.* ALEXANDRA *leans down, puts her cheek on* BIRDIE'S *arm.*)

ALEXANDRA

(*To* BIRDIE)

I guess we were all trying to make a happy day. You know, we sit around and try to pretend nothing's happened. We try to pretend we are not here. We make believe we are just by ourselves, some place else, and it doesn't seem to work. (*Kisses*

BIRDIE's *hand*) Come now, Aunt Birdie, I'll walk you home. You and me. (*She takes* BIRDIE's *arm. They move slowly out.*)

BIRDIE

(*Softly as they exit*)

You and me.

ADDIE

(*After a minute*)

Well. First time I ever heard Miss Birdie say a word. (HORACE *looks at her*) Maybe it's good for her. I'm just sorry Zan had to hear it. (HORACE *moves his head as if he were uncomfortable*) You feel bad, don't you? (*He shrugs.*)

HORACE

So you didn't want Zan to hear? It would be nice to let her stay innocent, like Birdie at her age. Let her listen now. Let her see everything. How else is she going to know that she's got to get away? I'm trying to show her that. I'm trying, but I've only got a little time left. She can even hate me when I'm dead, if she'll only learn to hate and fear this.

ADDIE

Mr. Horace—

HORACE

Pretty soon there'll be nobody to help her but you.

ADDIE

(*Crossing to him*)

What can I do?

HORACE

Take her away.

ADDIE

How can I do that? Do you think they'd let me just go away with her?

HORACE

I'll fix it so they can't stop you when you're ready to go. You'll go, Addie?

ADDIE

(*After a second, softly*)

Yes, sir. I promise. (*He touches her arm, nods.*)

HORACE

(*Quietly*)

I'm going to have Sol Fowler make me a new will. They'll make trouble, but you make Zan stand firm and Fowler'll do the rest. Addie, I'd like to leave you something for yourself. I always wanted to.

ADDIE

(*Laughs*)

Don't you do that, Mr. Horace. A nigger woman in a white man's will! I'd never get it nohow.

HORACE

I know. But upstairs in the armoire drawer there's seventeen hundred dollar bills. It's money left from my trip. It's in an envelope with your name. It's for you.

ADDIE

Seventeen hundred dollar bills! My God, Mr. Horace, I won't know how to count up that high. (*Shyly*) It's mighty kind and good of you. I don't know what to say for thanks—

CAL

(*Appears in doorway*)

I'm back. (*No answer*) I'm back.

ADDIE

So we see.

HORACE

Well?

CAL

Nothing. I just went down and spoke my piece. Just like you told me. I say, "Mr. Horace he thank you mightily for the safe box arriving in good shape and he say you come right after supper to his house and bring Mr. Attorney-at-law Sol Fowler with you." Then I wipe my hands on my coat. Every time I ever told a lie in my whole life, I wipe my hands right after. Can't help doing it. Well, while I'm wiping my hands, Mr. Leo jump up and say to me, "What box? What you talking about?"

HORACE

(*Smiles*)

Did he?

CAL

And Mr. Leo say he got to leave a little early cause he got something to do. And then Mr. Manders say Mr. Leo should sit right down and finish up his work and stop acting like somebody made him Mr. President. So he sit down. Now, just like I told you, Mr. Manders was mighty surprised with the message because he knows right well he brought the box— (*Points to box, sighs*) But he took it all right. Some men take everything easy and some do not.

HORACE

(*Puts his head back, laughs*)

Mr. Leo was telling the truth; he *has* got something to do. I hope Manders don't keep him too long. (*Outside there is the sound of voices.* CAL *exits.* ADDIE *crosses quickly to* HORACE, *puts basket on table, begins to wheel his chair towards the stairs. Sharply*) No. Leave me where I am.

ADDIE

But that's Miss Regina coming back.

HORACE

(*Nods, looking at door*)

Go away, Addie.

ADDIE

(*Hesitates*)

Mr. Horace. Don't talk no more today. You don't feel well and it won't do no good—

HORACE

(*As he hears footsteps in the hall*)

Go on. (*She looks at him for a second, then picks up her sewing from table and exits as* REGINA *comes in from hall.* HORACE'S *chair is now so placed that he is in front of the table with the medicine.* REGINA *stands in the hall, shakes umbrella, stands it in the corner, takes off her cloak and throws it over the banister. She stares at* HORACE.)

REGINA

(*As she takes off her gloves*)

We had agreed that you were to stay in your part of this

house and I in mine. This room is *my* part of the house. Please don't come down here again.

HORACE

I won't.

REGINA

(*Crosses towards bell-cord*)

I'll get Cal to take you upstairs.

HORACE

(*Smiles*)

Before you do I want to tell you that after all, we have invested our money in Hubbard Sons and Marshall, Cotton Manufacturers.

REGINA

(*Stops, turns, stares at him*)

What are you talking about? You haven't seen Ben— When did you change your mind?

HORACE

I didn't change my mind. *I* didn't invest the money. (*Smiles*) It was invested for me.

REGINA

(*Angrily*)

What—?

HORACE

I had eighty-eight thousand dollars' worth of Union Pacific bonds in that safe-deposit box. They are not there now. Go and look. (*As she stares at him, he points to the box*) Go and look, Regina. (*She crosses quickly to the box, opens it*) Those bonds are as negotiable as money.

REGINA

(*Turns back to him*)

What kind of joke are you playing now? Is this for my benefit?

HORACE

I don't look in that box very often, but three days ago, on Wednesday it was, because I had made a decision—

REGINA

I want to know what you are talking about.

HORACE

(*Sharply*)

Don't interrupt me again. Because I had made a decision, I sent for the box. The bonds were gone. Eighty-eight thousand dollars gone. (*He smiles at her.*)

REGINA

(*After a moment's silence, quietly*)

Do you think I'm crazy enough to believe what you're saying?

HORACE

(*Shrugs*)

Believe anything you like.

REGINA

(*Stares at him, slowly*)

Where did they go to?

HORACE

They are in Chicago. With Mr. Marshall, I should guess.

REGINA

What did they do? Walk to Chicago? Have you really gone crazy?

HORACE

Leo took the bonds.

REGINA

(*Turns sharply then speaks softly, without conviction*)
I don't believe it.

HORACE

(*Leans forward*)

I wasn't there but I can guess what happened. This fine gentleman, to whom you were willing to marry your daughter, took the keys and opened the box. You remember that the day of the fight Oscar went to Chicago? Well, he went with my bonds that his son Leo had stolen for him. (*Pleasantly*) And for Ben, of course, too.

REGINA

(*Slowly, nods*)

When did you find out the bonds were gone?

HORACE

Wednesday night.

REGINA

I thought that's what you said. Why have you waited three days to do anything? (*Suddenly laughs*) This *will* make a fine story.

HORACE

(*Nods*)

Couldn't it?

REGINA

(*Still laughing*)

A fine story to hold over their heads. How could they be such fools? (*Turns to him.*)

HORACE

But I'm not going to hold it over their heads.

REGINA

(*The laugh stops*)

What?

HORACE

(*Turns his chair to face her*)

I'm going to let them keep the bonds—as a loan from you. An eighty-eight-thousand-dollar loan; they should be grateful to you. They will be, I think.

REGINA

(*Slowly, smiles*)

I see. You are punishing me. But I won't let you punish me. If you won't do anything, I will. Now. (*She starts for door.*)

HORACE

You won't do anything. Because you can't. (REGINA *stops*) It won't do you any good to make trouble because I shall simply say that I lent them the bonds.

REGINA

(*Slowly*)

You would do that?

HORACE

Yes. For once in your life I am tying your hands. There is nothing for you to do. (*There is silence. Then she sits down.*)

REGINA

I see. You are going to lend them the bonds and let them keep all the profit they make on them, and there is nothing I can do about it. Is that right?

HORACE

Yes.

REGINA

(*Softly*)

Why did you say that I was making this gift?

HORACE

I was coming to that. I am going to make a new will, Regina, leaving you eighty-eight thousand dollars in Union Pacific bonds. The rest will go to Zan. It's true that your brothers have borrowed your share for a little while. After my death I advise you to talk to Ben and Oscar. They won't admit anything and Ben, I think, will be smart enough to see that he's safe. Because I knew about the theft and said nothing. Nor will I say anything as long as I live. Is that clear to you?

REGINA

(*Nods, softly, without looking at him*)

You will not say anything as long as you live.

HORACE

That's right. And by that time they will probably have replaced your bonds, and then they'll belong to you and nobody but us will ever know what happened. (*Stops, smiles*) They'll be around any minute to see what I am going to do. I took good care to see that word reached Leo. They'll be mighty relieved to know I'm going to do nothing and Ben will think it all a capital joke on you. And that will be the end of that. There's nothing you can do to them, nothing you can do to me.

REGINA

You hate me very much.

HORACE

No.

REGINA

Oh, I think you do. (*Puts her head back, sighs*) Well, we haven't been very good together. Anyway, I don't hate you either. I have only contempt for you. I've always had.

HORACE

From the very first?

REGINA

I think so.

HORACE

I was in love with *you*. But why did *you* marry *me?*

REGINA

I was lonely when I was young.

HORACE

You were lonely?

REGINA

Not the way people usually mean. Lonely for all the things I wasn't going to get. Everybody in this house was so busy and there was so little place for what I wanted. I wanted the world. Then, and then— (*Smiles*) Papa died and left the money to Ben and Oscar.

HORACE

And you married me?

REGINA

Yes, I thought— But I was wrong. You were a small-town clerk then. You haven't changed.

HORACE

(*Nods, smiles*)

And that wasn't what you wanted.

REGINA

No. No, it wasn't what I wanted. (*Pauses, leans back, pleasantly*) It took me a little while to find out I had made a mistake. As for you—I don't know. It was almost as if I couldn't stand the kind of man you were— (*Smiles, softly*) I used to lie there at night, praying you wouldn't come near—

HORACE

Really? It was as bad as that?

REGINA

(*Nods*)

Remember when I went to Doctor Sloan and I told you

he said there was something the matter with me and that you shouldn't touch me any more?

HORACE

I remember.

REGINA

But you believed it. I couldn't understand that. I couldn't understand that anybody could be such a soft fool. That was when I began to despise you.

HORACE

(*Puts his hand to his throat, looks at the bottle of medicine on table*)

Why didn't you leave me?

REGINA

I told you I married you for something. It turned out it was only for this. (*Carefully*) This wasn't what I wanted, but it was something. I never thought about it much but if I had (HORACE *puts his hand to his throat*) I'd have known that you would die before I would. But I couldn't have known that you would get heart trouble so early and so bad. I'm lucky, Horace. I've always been lucky. (HORACE *turns slowly to the medicine*) I'll be lucky again. (HORACE *looks at her. Then he puts his hand to his throat. Because he cannot reach the bottle he moves the chair closer. He reaches for the medicine, takes out the cork, picks up the spoon. The bottle slips and smashes on the table. He draws in his breath, gasps.*)

HORACE

Please. Tell Addie— The other bottle is upstairs. (REGINA *has not moved. She does not move now. He stares at her. Then, suddenly as if he understood, he raises his voice. It is a panic-stricken whisper, too small to be heard outside the room)* Addie! Addie! Come— (*Stops as he hears the softness of his voice. He makes a sudden, furious spring from the chair to the stairs, taking the first few steps as if he were a desperate runner. On the fourth step he slips, gasps, grasps the rail, makes a great effort to reach the landing. When he reaches the landing, he is on his knees. His knees give way, he falls on the landing, out of view.* REGINA *has not turned during his climb up the stairs. Now she waits a second. Then she goes below the landing, speaks up*)

REGINA

Horace. Horace. (*When there is no answer, she turns, calls*) Addie! Cal! Come in here. (*She starts up the steps.* ADDIE *and* CAL *appear. Both run towards the stairs*) He's had an attack. Come up here. (*They run up the steps quickly.*)

CAL

My God. Mr. Horace—
(*They cannot be seen now.*)

REGINA

(*Her voice comes from the head of the stairs*)
Be still, Cal. Bring him in here.
(*Before the footsteps and the voices have completely died away,* ALEXANDRA *appears in the hall door, in her raincloak and hood. She comes into the room, begins to unfasten the cloak, suddenly looks around, sees the empty wheel chair, stares, begins to move swiftly as*

if to look in the dining room. At the same moment ADDIE *runs down the stairs.* ALEXANDRA *turns and stares up at* ADDIE.)

ALEXANDRA

Addie! What?

ADDIE

(*Takes* ALEXANDRA *by the shoulders*)

I'm going for the doctor. Go upstairs. (ALEXANDRA *looks at her, then quickly breaks away and runs up the steps.* ADDIE *exits. The stage is empty for a minute. Then the front door bell begins to ring. When there is no answer, it rings again. A second later* LEO *appears in the hall, talking as he comes in.*)

LEO

(*Very nervous*)

Hello. (*Irritably*) Never saw any use ringing a bell when a door was open. If you are going to ring a bell, then somebody should answer it. (*Gets in the room, looks around, puzzled, listens, hears no sound*) Aunt Regina. (*He moves around restlessly*) Addie. (*Waits*) Where the hell— (*Crosses to the bell cord, rings it impatiently, waits, gets no answer, calls*) Call! Cal! (CAL *appears on the stair landing.*)

CAL

(*His voice is soft, shaken*)

Mr. Leo. Miss Regina says you stop that screaming noise.

LEO

(*Angrily*)

Where is everybody?

CAL

Mr. Horace he got an attack. He's bad. Miss Regina says you stop that noise.

LEO

Uncle Horace— What— What happened? (CAL *starts down the stairs, shakes his head, begins to move swiftly off.* LEO *looks around wildly*) But when— You seen Mr. Oscar or Mr. Ben? (CAL *shakes his head. Moves on.* LEO *grabs him by the arm*) Answer me, will you?

CAL

No, I ain't seen 'em. I ain't got time to answer you. I got to get things. (CAL *runs off.*)

LEO

But what's the matter with him? When did this happen— (*Calling after* CAL) You'd think Papa'd be some place where you could find him. I been chasing him all afternoon.

(OSCAR *and* BEN *come into the room, talking excitedly.*)

OSCAR

I hope it's not a bad attack.

BEN

It's the first one he's had since he came home.

LEO

Papa, I've been looking all over town for you and Uncle Ben—

BEN

Where is he?

OSCAR

Addie said it was sudden.

BEN

(*To* LEO)

Where is he? When did it happen?

LEO

Upstairs. Will you listen to me, please? I been looking for you for—

OSCAR

(*To* BEN)

You think we should go up? (BEN, *looking up the steps, shakes his head.*)

BEN

I don't know. I don't know.

OSCAR

(*Shakes his head*)

But he was all right—

LEO

(*Yelling*)

Will you listen to me?

OSCAR

(*Sharply*)

What is the matter with you?

LEO

I been trying to tell you. I been trying to find you for an hour—

OSCAR

Tell me what?

LEO

Uncle Horace knows about the bonds. He knows about them. He's had the box since Wednesday—

BEN

(*Sharply*)

Stop shouting! What the hell are you talking about?

LEO

(*Furiously*)

I'm telling you he knows about the bonds. Ain't that clear enough—

OSCAR

(*Grabbing* LEO's *arm*)

You God-damn fool! Stop screaming!

BEN

Now what happened? Talk quietly.

LEO

You heard me. Uncle Horace knows about the bonds. He's known since Wednesday.

BEN

(*After a second*)

How do you know that?

LEO

Because Cal comes down to Manders and says the box came O.K. and—

OSCAR

(*Trembling*)

That might not mean a thing—

LEO

(*Angrily*)

No? It might not, huh? Then he says Manders should come here tonight and bring Sol Fowler with him. I guess that don't mean a thing either.

OSCAR

(*To* BEN)

Ben— What— Do you think he's seen the—

BEN

(*Motions to the box*)

There's the box. (*Both* OSCAR *and* LEO *turn sharply.* LEO *makes a leap to the box*) You ass. Put it down. What are you going to do with it, eat it?

LEO

I'm going to— (*Starts.*)

BEN

(*Furiously*)

Put it down. Don't touch it again. Now sit down and shut up for a minute.

OSCAR

Since Wednesday. (*To* LEO) You said he had it since Wednesday. Why didn't he say something— (*To* BEN) I don't understand—

LEO

(*Taking a step*)

I can put it back. I can put it back before anybody knows.

BEN

(*Who is standing at the table, softly*)

He's had it since Wednesday. Yet he hasn't said a word to us.

OSCAR

Why? Why?

LEO

What's the difference why? He was getting ready to say plenty. He was going to say it to Fowler tonight—

OSCAR

(*Angrily*)

Be still. (*Turns to* BEN, *looks at him, waits.*)

BEN

(*After a minute*)

I don't believe that.

LEO

(*Wildly*)

You don't believe it? What do I care what *you* believe? I do the dirty work and then—

BEN

(*Turning his head sharply to* LEO)

I'm remembering that. I'm remembering that, Leo.

OSCAR

What do you mean?

LEO

You—

BEN

(*To* OSCAR)

If you don't shut that little fool up, I'll show you what I mean. For some reason he knows, but he don't say a word.

OSCAR

Maybe he didn't know that *we*—

BEN

(*Quickly*)

That *Leo*— He's no fool. Does Manders know the bonds are missing?

LEO

How could I tell? I was half crazy. I don't think so. Because Manders seemed kind of puzzled and—

OSCAR

But we got to find out— (*He breaks off as* CAL *comes into the room carrying a kettle of hot water.*)

BEN

How is he, Cal?

CAL

I don't know, Mr. Ben. He was bad. (*Going towards stairs.*)

OSCAR

But when did it happen?

CAL

(*Shrugs*)

He wasn't feeling bad early. (ADDIE *comes in quickly from the hall*) Then there he is next thing on the landing, fallen over, his eyes tight—

ADDIE

(*To* CAL)

Dr. Sloan's over at the Ballongs. Hitch the buggy and go get him. (*She takes the kettle and cloths from him, pushes him, runs up the stairs*) Go on. (*She disappears.* CAL *exits.*)

BEN

Never seen Sloan anywhere when you need him.

OSCAR

(*Softly*)

Sounds bad.

LEO

He would have told *her* about it. Aunt Regina. He would have told his own wife—

BEN

(*Turning to* LEO)

Yes, he might have told her. But they weren't on such pretty terms and maybe he didn't. Maybe he didn't. (*Goes quickly to* LEO) Now, listen to me. If she doesn't know, it may work out all right. If she does know, you're to say he lent you the bonds.

LEO

Lent them to me! Who's going to believe that?

BEN

Nobody.

OSCAR

(*To* LEO)

Don't you understand? It can't do no harm to say it—

LEO

Why should I say he lent them to me? Why not to you? (*Carefully*) Why not to Uncle Ben?

BEN

(*Smiles*)

Just because he didn't lend them to me. Remember that.

LEO

But all he has to do is say he didn't lend them to me—

BEN

(*Furiously*)

But for some reason, he doesn't seem to be talking, does he?

(*There are footsteps above. They all stand looking at the stairs.* REGINA *begins to come slowly down.*)

BEN

What happened?

REGINA

He's had a bad attack.

OSCAR

Too bad. I'm so sorry we weren't here when—when Horace needed us.

BEN

When *you* needed us.

REGINA

(*Looks at him*)

Yes.

BEN

How is he? Can we—can we go up?

REGINA

(*Shakes her head*)

He's not conscious.

OSCAR

(*Pacing around*)

It's that—it's that bad? Wouldn't you think Sloan could be found quickly, just once, just once?

REGINA

I don't think there is much for him to do.

BEN

Oh, don't talk like that. He's come through attacks before. He will now.

(REGINA *sits down. After a second she speaks softly.*)

REGINA

Well. We haven't seen each other since the day of our fight.

BEN

(*Tenderly*)

That was nothing. Why, you and Oscar and I used to fight when we were kids.

OSCAR

(*Hurriedly*)

Don't you think we should go up? Is there anything we can do for Horace—

BEN

You don't feel well. Ah—

REGINA

(*Without looking at them*)

No, I don't. (*Slight pause*) Horace told me about the bonds this afternoon. (*There is an immediate shocked silence.*)

LEO

The bonds. What do you mean? What bonds? What—

BEN

(*Looks at him furiously. Then to* REGINA)

The Union Pacific bonds? *Horace's* Union Pacific bonds?

REGINA

Yes.

OSCAR

(*Steps to her, very nervously*)

Well. Well what—what about them? What—what could he say?

REGINA

He said that Leo had stolen the bonds and given them to you.

OSCAR

(*Aghast, very loudly*)

That's ridiculous, Regina, absolutely—

LEO

I don't know what you're talking about. What would I— Why—

REGINA

(*Wearily to* BEN)

Isn't it enough that he stole them from me? Do I have to listen to this in the bargain?

OSCAR

You are talking—

LEO

I didn't steal anything. I don't know why—

REGINA

(*To* BEN)

Would you ask them to stop that, please? (*There is silence for a minute.* BEN *glowers at* OSCAR *and* LEO.)

BEN

Aren't we starting at the wrong end, Regina? What did Horace tell you?

REGINA

(*Smiles at him*)

He told me that Leo had stolen the bonds.

LEO

I didn't steal—

REGINA

Please. Let me finish. Then he told me that he was going to pretend that he had lent them to you (LEO *turns sharply to* REGINA, *then looks at* OSCAR, *then looks back at* REGINA) as a present from me—to my brothers. He said there was nothing I could do about it. He said the rest of his money would go to Alexandra. That is all. (*There is a silence.* OSCAR *coughs,* LEO *smiles slyly.*)

LEO

(*Taking a step to her*)

I told you he had lent them— I could have told you—

REGINA

(*Ignores him, smiles sadly at* BEN)

So I'm very badly off, you see. (*Carefully*) But Horace said there was nothing I could do about it as long as he was alive to say he had lent you the bonds.

BEN

You shouldn't feel that way. It can all be explained, all be adjusted. It isn't as bad—

REGINA

So you, at least, are willing to admit that the bonds were stolen?

BEN

(OSCAR *laughs nervously*)

I admit no such thing. It's possible that Horace made up that part of the story to tease you— (*Looks at her*) Or perhaps to punish you. Punish you.

REGINA

(*Sadly*)

It's not a pleasant story. I feel bad, Ben, naturally. I hadn't thought—

BEN

Now you shall have the bonds safely back. That was the understanding, wasn't it, Oscar?

OSCAR

Yes.

REGINA

I'm glad to know that. (*Smiles*) Ah, I had greater hopes—

BEN

Don't talk that way. That's foolish. (*Looks at his watch*) I think we ought to drive out for Sloan ourselves. If we can't find him we'll go over to Senateville for Doctor Morris. And don't think I'm dismissing this other business. I'm not. We'll have it all out on a more appropriate day.

REGINA

(*Looks up, quietly*)

I don't think you had better go yet. I think you had better stay and sit down.

BEN

We'll be back with Sloan.

REGINA

Cal has gone for him. I don't want you to go.

BEN

Now don't worry and—

REGINA

You will come back in this room and sit down. I have something more to say.

BEN

(*Turns, comes towards her*)

Since when do I take orders from you?

REGINA

(*Smiles*)

You don't—yet. (*Sharply*) Come back, Oscar. You too, Leo.

OSCAR

(*Sure of himself, laughs*)

My dear Regina—

BEN

(*Softly, pats her hand*)

Horace has already clipped your wings and very wittily. Do I have to clip them, too? (*Smiles at her*) You'd get farther with a smile, Regina. I'm a soft man for a woman's smile.

REGINA

I'm smiling, Ben. I'm smiling because you are quite safe while Horace lives. But I don't think Horace will live. And if he doesn't live I shall want seventy-five per cent in exchange for the bonds.

BEN

(*Steps back, whistles, laughs*)

Greedy! What a greedy girl you are! You want so much of everything.

REGINA

Yes. And if I don't get what I want I am going to put all three of you in jail.

OSCAR

(*Furiously*)

You're mighty crazy. Having just admitted—

BEN

And on what evidence would you put Oscar and Leo in jail?

REGINA

(*Laughs, gaily*)

Oscar, listen to him. He's getting ready to swear that it was you and Leo! What do you say to that? (OSCAR *turns furiously towards* BEN) Oh, don't be angry, Oscar. I'm going to see that he goes in with you.

BEN

Try anything you like, Regina. (*Sharply*) And now we can stop all this and say good-bye to you. (ALEXANDRA *comes slowly down the steps*) It's his money and he's obviously willing to let us borrow it. (*More pleasantly*) Learn to make threats when you can carry them through. For how many years have I told you a good-looking woman gets more by being soft and appealing? Mama used to tell you that. (*Looks at his watch*) Where the hell is Sloan? (*To* OSCAR) Take the buggy and— (*As* BEN *turns to* OSCAR, *he sees* ALEXANDRA. *She walks stiffly. She goes slowly to the lower window, her head bent. They all turn to look at her.*)

OSCAR

(*After a second, moving toward her*)

What? Alexandra— (*She does not answer. After a second,* ADDIE *comes slowly down the stairs, moving as if she were very tired. At foot of steps, she looks at* ALEXANDRA, *then turns and slowly crosses to door and exits.* REGINA *rises.* BEN *looks nervously at* ALEXANDRA, *at* REGINA.)

OSCAR

(*As* ADDIE *passes him, irritably to* ALEXANDRA)

Well, what is— (*Turns into room—sees* ADDIE *at foot of steps*) —what's? (BEN *puts up a hand, shakes his head*) My God, I didn't know—who *could* have known—I didn't know he was that sick. Well, well—I— (REGINA *stands quietly, her back to them.*)

BEN

(*Softly, sincerely*)

Seems like yesterday when he first came here.

OSCAR

(*Sincerely, nervously*)

Yes, that's true. (*Turns to* BEN) The whole town loved him and respected him.

ALEXANDRA

(*Turns*)

Did you love him, Uncle Oscar?

OSCAR

Certainly, I— What a strange thing to ask! I—

ALEXANDRA

Did you love him, Uncle Ben?

BEN

(*Simply*)

He had—

ALEXANDRA

(*Suddenly starts to laugh very loudly*)

And you, Mama, did you love him, too?

REGINA

I know what you feel, Alexandra, but please try to control yourself.

ALEXANDRA

(*Still laughing*)

I'm trying, Mama. I'm trying very hard.

BEN

Grief makes some people laugh and some people cry. It's better to cry, Alexandra.

ALEXANDRA

(*The laugh has stopped. Tensely moves toward* REGINA)

What was Papa doing on the staircase?

(BEN *turns to look at* ALEXANDRA.)

REGINA

Please go and lie down, my dear. We all need time to get over shocks like this. (ALEXANDRA *does not move.* REGINA'S *voice becomes softer, more insistent*) Please go, Alexandra.

ALEXANDRA

No, Mama. I'll wait. I've got to talk to you.

REGINA

Later. Go and rest now.

ALEXANDRA

(Quietly)

I'll wait, Mama. I've plenty of time.

REGINA

(Hesitates, stares, makes a half shrug, turns back to BEN*)*

As I was saying. Tomorrow morning I am going up to Judge Simmes. I shall tell him about Leo.

BEN

(Motioning toward ALEXANDRA*)*

Not in front of the child, Regina. I—

REGINA

(Turns to him. Sharply)

I didn't ask her to stay. Tomorrow morning I go to Judge Simmes—

OSCAR

And what proof? What proof of all this—

REGINA

(Turns sharply)

None. I won't need any. The bonds are missing and they are with Marshall. That will be enough. If it isn't, I'll add what's necessary.

BEN

I'm sure of that.

REGINA

(*Turns to* BEN)

You can be quite sure.

OSCAR

We'll deny—

REGINA

Deny your heads off. You couldn't find a jury that wouldn't weep for a woman whose brothers steal from her. And you couldn't find twelve men in this state you haven't cheated and hate you for it.

OSCAR

What kind of talk is this? You couldn't do anything like that! We're your own brothers. (*Points upstairs*) How can you talk that way when upstairs not five minutes ago—

REGINA

(*Slowly*)

There are people who can never go back, who must finish what they start. I am one of those people, Oscar. (*After a slight pause*) Where was I? (*Smiles at* BEN) Well, they'll convict you. But I won't care much if they don't. (*Leans forward, pleasantly*) Because by that time you'll be ruined. I shall also tell my story to Mr. Marshall, who likes me, I think, and who will not want to be involved in your scandal. A respectable firm like Marshall and Company. The deal would be off in an hour. (*Turns to them angrily*) And you know it. Now I don't want to hear any more from any of you. *You'll do no more bargaining in this house.* I'll take my seventy-five per cent and we'll forget the story forever. That's one way of doing it, and the way I prefer. You know me well enough to know that I don't mind taking the other way.

BEN

(*After a second, slowly*)

None of us have ever known you well enough, Regina.

REGINA

You're getting old, Ben. Your tricks aren't as smart as they used to be. (*There is no answer. She waits, then smiles*) All right. I take it that's settled and I get what I asked for.

OSCAR

(*Furiously to* BEN)

Are you going to let her do this—

BEN

(*Turns to look at him, slowly*)

You have a suggestion?

REGINA

(*Puts her arms above her head, stretches, laughs*)

No, he hasn't. All right. Now, Leo, I have forgotten that you ever saw the bonds. (*Archly, to* BEN *and* OSCAR) And as long as you boys both behave yourselves, I've forgotten that we ever talked about them. You can draw up the necessary papers tomorrow. (BEN *laughs.* LEO *stares at him, starts for door. Exits.* OSCAR *moves towards door angrily.* REGINA *looks at* BEN, *nods, laughs with him. For a second,* OSCAR *stands in the door, looking back at them. Then he exits.*)

REGINA

You're a good loser, Ben. I like that.

BEN

(*He picks up his coat, then turns to her*)

Well, I say to myself, what's the good? You and I aren't like Oscar. We're not sour people. I think that comes from a good digestion. Then, too, one loses today and wins tomorrow. I say to myself, years of planning and I get what I want. Then I don't get it. But I'm not discouraged. The century's turning, the world is open. Open for people like you and me. Ready for us, waiting for us. After all this is just the beginning. There are hundreds of Hubbards sitting in rooms like this throughout the country. All their names aren't Hubbard, but they are all Hubbards and they will own this country some day. We'll get along.

REGINA

(*Smiles*)

I think so.

BEN

Then, too, I say to myself, things may change. (*Looks at* ALEXANDRA) I agree with Alexandra. What is a man in a wheel chair doing on a staircase? I ask myself that.

REGINA

(*Looks up at him*)

And what do you answer?

BEN

I have no answer. But maybe some day I will. Maybe never,

but maybe some day. (*Smiles. Pats her arm*) When I do, I'll let you know. (*Goes towards hall.*)

REGINA

When you do, write me. I will be in Chicago. (*Gaily*) Ah, Ben, if Papa had only left me his money.

BEN

I'll see you tomorrow.

REGINA

Oh, yes. Certainly. You'll be sort of working for me now.

BEN

(*As he passes* ALEXANDRA, *smiles*)

Alexandra, you're turning out to be a right interesting girl. (*Looks at* REGINA) Well, good night all. (*He exits.*)

REGINA

(*Sits quietly for a second, stretches, turns to look at* ALEXANDRA)

What do you want to talk to me about, Alexandra?

ALEXANDRA

(*Slowly*)

I've changed my mind. I don't want to talk. There's nothing to talk about now.

REGINA

You're acting very strange. Not like yourself. You've had a bad shock today. I know that. And you loved Papa, but you must have expected this to come some day. You knew how sick he was.

ALEXANDRA

I knew. We all knew.

REGINA

It will be good for you to get away from here. Good for me, too. Time heals most wounds, Alexandra. You're young, you shall have all the things I wanted. I'll make the world for you the way I wanted it to be for me. (*Uncomfortably*) Don't sit there staring. You've been around Birdie so much you're getting just like her.

ALEXANDRA

(*Nods*)

Funny. That's what Aunt Birdie said today.

REGINA

(*Nods*)

Be good for you to get away from all this.

(ADDIE *enters.*)

ADDIE

Cal is back, Miss Regina. He says Dr. Sloan will be coming in a few minutes.

REGINA

We'll go in a few weeks. A few weeks! That means two or three Saturdays, two or three Sundays. (*Sighs*) Well, I'm very tired. I shall go to bed. I don't want any supper. Put the lights out and lock up. (ADDIE *moves to the piano lamp, turns it out*) You go to your room, Alexandra. Addie will bring you something hot. You look very tired. (*Rises. To* ADDIE) Call me when Dr. Sloan gets here. I don't want to see anybody else. I don't want any condolence calls tonight. The whole town will be over.

ALEXANDRA

Mama, I'm not coming with you. I'm not going to Chicago.

REGINA

(*Turns to her*)

You're very upset, Alexandra.

ALEXANDRA

(*Quietly*)

I mean what I say. With all my heart.

REGINA

We'll talk about it tomorrow. The morning will make a difference.

ALEXANDRA

It won't make any difference. And there isn't anything to talk about. I am going away from you. Because I want to. Because I know Papa would want me to.

REGINA

(*Puzzled, careful, polite*)

You *know* your papa wanted you to go away from me?

ALEXANDRA

Yes.

REGINA

(*Softly*)

And if I say no?

ALEXANDRA

(*Looks at her*)

Say it, Mama, say it. And see what happens.

REGINA

(*Softly, after a pause*)

And if I make you stay?

ALEXANDRA

That would be foolish. It wouldn't work in the end.

REGINA

You're very serious about it, aren't you? (*Crosses to stairs*) Well, you'll change your mind in a few days.

ALEXANDRA

You only change your mind when you want to. And I won't want to.

REGINA

(*Going up the steps*)

Alexandra, I've come to the end of my rope. Somewhere there has to be what I want, too. Life goes too fast. Do what you want; think what you want; go where you want. I'd like to keep you with me, but I won't make you stay. Too many people used to make me do too many things. No, I won't make you stay.

ALEXANDRA

You couldn't, Mama, because I want to leave here. As I've never wanted anything in my life before. Because now I understand what Papa was trying to tell me. (*Pause*) All in one day: Addie said there were people who ate the earth and other people who stood around and watched them do it. And just now Uncle Ben said the same thing. Really, he said the same thing. (*Tensely*) Well, tell him for me, Mama, I'm not going to stand around and watch you do it. Tell him I'll be fighting as hard as he'll be fighting (*Rises*) some place where people don't just stand around and watch.

REGINA

Well, you have spirit, after all. I used to think you were all sugar water. We don't have to be bad friends. I don't want us to be bad friends, Alexandra. (*Starts, stops, turns to* ALEXANDRA) Would you like to come and talk to me, Alexandra? Would you—would you like to sleep in my room tonight?

ALEXANDRA

(*Takes a step towards her*)

Are you afraid, Mama? (REGINA *does not answer. She moves slowly out of sight.* ADDIE *comes to* ALEXANDRA, *presses her arm.*)

The Curtain Falls

Another Part of the Forest

For my good friend

GREGORY ZILBOORG

Another Part of the Forest was first produced at the Fulton Theatre, New York City, on November 20, 1946, with the following cast:

REGINA HUBBARD	Patricia Neal
JOHN BAGTRY	Bartlett Robinson
LAVINIA HUBBARD	Mildred Dunnock
CORALEE	Beatrice Thompson
MARCUS HUBBARD	Percy Waram
BENJAMIN HUBBARD	Leo Genn
JACOB	Stanley Greene
OSCAR HUBBARD	Scott McKay
SIMON ISHAM	Owen Coll
BIRDIE BAGTRY	Margaret Phillips
HAROLD PENNIMAN	Paul Ford
GILBERT JUGGER	Gene O'Donnell
LAURETTE SINCEE	Jean Hagen

Produced by Kermit Bloomgarden
Directed by Lillian Hellman
Settings designed by Jo Mielziner

SYNOPSIS OF SCENES

ACT ONE: *A Sunday morning in June 1880, the Alabama town of Bowden, the side portico of the Hubbard house.*

ACT TWO: *The next evening, the living room of the Hubbard house.*

ACT THREE: *Early the next morning, the side portico of the Hubbard house.*

Throughout the play, in the stage directions, left and right mean audience's left and right.

Act One

SCENE: *The side portico of the Hubbard house, a Sunday morning in the summer of 1880 in the Alabama town of Bowden. The portico leads into the living room by back center French doors. On the right side of the portico is an old wing of the house. An exterior staircase to this wing leads to an upper porch off which are the bedrooms of the house and behind the staircase are the back gardens and the kitchen quarters. Under the second-story porch is a door leading to the dining room of the house, and a back door leading to the kitchen. The other side of the portico leads to a lawn which faces the town's main street. The main part of the house, built in the 1850's, is Southern Greek. It is not a great mansion but it is a good house built by a man of taste from whom Marcus Hubbard bought it after the Civil War. There is not much furniture on the portico: two chairs and a table at one end, one comfortable chair and a table at the other end. Twin heads of Aristotle are on high pedestals. There is something too austere, too pretended Greek about the portico, as if it followed one man's eccentric taste and was not designed to be comfortable for anyone else.*

As the curtain rises, Regina Hubbard, a handsome girl of twenty, is standing looking down at John Bagtry. Regina has on a pretty negligee thrown over a nightgown. Her hair is pinned high, as if she had pinned it up quickly. John Bagtry is a man of thirty-six with a sad, worn face. He is dressed in shabby riding shirt and Confederate Cavalry pants.

REGINA, *after a long silence:* Where were you going?

JOHN, *he has a soft, easy voice:* And what you doing awake so early?

REGINA: Watching for you. But you tried not to hear me when I called you. I called you three times before you turned.

JOHN: I didn't think this was the place or the hour for us to be meeting together. *Looks around nervously.* We'll be waking your folks. You out here in your wrapper! That would make a pretty scandal, honey—

REGINA, *impatiently:* Nobody's awake. And I don't care. Why didn't you—

JOHN, *quickly, gaily:* Oh, your Mama's up all right. I saw her and your Coralee going into nigger church. I bowed to her—

REGINA, *softly:* Why didn't you meet me last night?

JOHN, *after a second:* I couldn't. And I didn't know how to send word.

REGINA: Why couldn't you? Plantation folks giving balls again? Or fancy dress parties?

JOHN, *smiles:* I haven't been to a party since I was sixteen years old, Regina. The Bacons gave the last ball I ever remember, to celebrate the opening of the war and say good-bye to us—

REGINA: You've told me about it. Why couldn't you come last night?

JOHN: I couldn't leave Aunt Clara and Cousin Birdie. They wanted to sit out and talk after supper, and I couldn't.

REGINA, *slowly:* They wanted to talk? And so they made you stay?

JOHN: No, they didn't *make* me. They're lonely, Regina, and I'm not with them much, since you and I—

REGINA: Why should you be with them? When I want to meet you, I go and do it.

JOHN: Things are different with us. Everything is bad. This summer is the worst, I guess, in all the years. They are lonely—

REGINA: It's not the first time you didn't come. And you think I shouldn't be angry, and take you back the next day. It would be better if you lied to me where you were. This way it's just insulting to me. Better if you lied.

JOHN: Lie? Why would I lie?

REGINA: Better if you said you were with another woman. But not meeting me because of those two mummies—

JOHN, *softly:* I like them, Regina. And they don't go around raising their voices in anger on an early Sunday day.

REGINA: I don't want you to tell me about the differences in your family and mine.

JOHN, *stares at her:* I've never done that. Never.

REGINA: That's what you always mean when you say I'm screaming.

JOHN, *sharply:* I mean no such thing. I said only that I stayed with Aunt Clara and Cousin Birdie last night. And I'll do it again. *Desperately:* Look, honey, I didn't mean not to come to meet you. But I've lived on them for fifteen years. They're good to me. They share with me the little they got, and I don't give back anything to them—

REGINA, *tensely:* I'm getting sick of them. They've got to know about you and me some day soon. I think I'm going to sashay right up to that sacred plantation grass and tell them the war's over, the old times are finished, and so are they. I'm going to tell them to stay out of my way—

JOHN, *sharply:* They've never mentioned you, Regina.

REGINA: That's good breeding: to know about something and not talk about it?

JOHN: I don't know about good breeding.

REGINA, *turns to him:* They think they do. Your Cousin Birdie's never done more than say good morning in all these years—when she knows full well who I am and who Papa is. Knows full well he could buy and sell Lionnet on the same morning, its cotton and its women with it—

JOHN, *takes her arm, very sharply:* I would not like to hear anybody talk that way again. No, I wouldn't.

REGINA, *pleadingly, softly:* I'm sorry, I'm sorry, I'm sorry. I give you my apology. I'm sorry, darling.

JOHN: We shouldn't be—

REGINA, *runs to him, takes his arm:* I'm never going to be mean again, never going to talk mean— Look, honey, I was mad about last night because I wanted to tell you about my plan. I've been thinking about it for months, and I've got Papa almost ready for it. But I can't tell it to you tonight because Papa makes me read to him every Sunday. But late tomorrow night, after Papa's music—it's over early—please, darling, tomorrow night—tomorrow night— *She clings to him.*

JOHN, *turns to her:* Regina, we mustn't. We mustn't any more. It's not right for you, honey, we're a scandal now. I'm no good for you. I'm too old, I'm—

REGINA, *clinging to him, impatient:* Why do you say that? A man at thirty-six talking that way? It comes from hanging around this town and your kinfolk.

JOHN: I was only good once—in a war. Some men shouldn't ever come home from a war. You know something? It's the only time I was happy.

REGINA, *draws away from him, wearily:* Oh, don't tell

me that again. You and your damn war. Wasn't it silly to be happy when you knew you were going to lose?

JOHN: You think it is silly? You think we all were? Of course you do. In this house you couldn't think anything else. *She draws back.* And now *I'm* sorry. That was most rude. It's late, honey.

REGINA, *quickly:* You haven't even asked me about my plan.

JOHN: I have a plan, too. I have a letter from Cod Carter. He's in Brazil. He's fighting down there, he says—

Lavinia Hubbard and Coralee appear from around the portico, as if coming from street. John stares at them, draws back nervously. Regina watches him, amused. Lavinia Hubbard is a woman of about fifty-eight, stooped, thin, delicate-looking. She has a sweet, high voice and a distracted, nervous way of speaking. Coralee is a sturdy Negro woman of about forty-five. She is holding a parasol over Lavinia. John steps forward. Coralee folds parasol, stares at Regina's costume, exits under porch to kitchen.

LAVINIA, *as if this were an ordinary morning scene:* Morning, Captain Bagtry. Been for a nice little stroll?

JOHN, *quickly:* Morning, Mrs. Hubbard. No, ma'am. I was just riding by and glimpsed Miss Regina—

LAVINIA, *nods:* That's nice. Coralee and I been to our church. The colored folks said a prayer for me and a little song. It's my birthday.

JOHN: Congratulations, ma'am. I sure give you my good wishes.

LAVINIA: Thank you, sir. And later I'm going back to the second service. And I know a secret: they're going to give me a cake. Ain't that lovely of them, and me undeserving? *Looks up at him:* I always go to the colored church. I ain't been to a white church in years. Most people don't like my doing it, I'm sure, but I got my good reasons—

REGINA: All right, Mama.

LAVINIA: There's got to be one little thing you do that you want to do, all by yourself you want to do it.

REGINA, *sharply:* All right, Mama.

LAVINIA, *hurries toward the doors of the living room:* Oh. Sorry. *At the door of living room, looks back at John:* I remember you and your cousins the day you left town for war. I blew you a kiss. Course we were living in our little house then and you didn't know. But I blew you all a kiss.

JOHN, *very pleased:* I'm glad to know it, ma'am. It was a great day. A hot day— You know something, ma'am? It was my birthday, too, that day. I was sixteen, and my cousins not much older. My birthday. Isn't that a coincidence, ma'am?

REGINA: Why?

JOHN, *lamely:* Because it's your Mama's birthday today.

LAVINIA: And you know something else, Captain Bagtry? Tomorrow's my wedding anniversary day. Your birthday, my birthday, and a wedding anniversary day.

REGINA, *very sharply:* All right, Mama.

Marcus Hubbard opens the door of his bedroom and appears on the upper porch. He is a strong-looking man of sixty-three, with a soft voice of tone and depth. He speaks slowly, as if he put value on the words.

MARCUS: Who's speaking on the porch?

At the sound of his voice Lavinia hurries into the house. John draws back into the living-room doors. Regina comes forward.

REGINA: I'm down here, Papa.

MARCUS: Morning, darling. Waiting for me?

REGINA: Er. Mama's just been to church.

MARCUS: Of course—where else would she go? Wait. Have your first coffee with me. *He exits into his room.*

REGINA, *amused at John's nervous movements, takes his arm:* I want you to meet Papa. Not now. But soon.

JOHN: I know your Papa. I'm in and out of your store—

REGINA: I want you to come *here.* I guess no Bagtry ever been inside our house. But would your Aunt Clara and your Cousin Birdie allow you to come, do you reckon?

JOHN: Allow me? I didn't think that was the way it was. I thought your Papa didn't want anybody here—

REGINA: He doesn't. But I'll find a way. Will you meet me tomorrow night, same place? Darling, darling, please. Please. *She pulls him toward her. He hesitates for a second. Then he takes her in his arms, kisses her with great feeling. She smiles.* Meet me?

JOHN, *softly:* I always do. No matter what I say or think, I always do.

He kisses her again. Then he runs off. She stands for a minute staring after him. Then, from the street side of the lawn, Benjamin Hubbard appears. He is followed by Jacob carrying a small valise and three boxes. Jacob is a tall, thin Negro of about thirty. Ben is thirty-five: a powerful, calm man with a quiet manner.

REGINA, *amused:* Morning, Ben. Have a good trip?

BEN: Was that Bagtry?

REGINA: He said that was his name.

BEN: What you doing having men on the porch, you in your wrapper?

REGINA, *gaily:* Isn't it a pretty wrapper? Came from Chicago.

BEN, *pointing to boxes:* And so did these, on the mail train. They got your name on 'em. Belong to you?

REGINA, *giggling:* Writing can't lie. Specially writing in ink.

MARCUS, *reappears on balcony, calls down:* Coffee ready for me, darling?

REGINA, *gaily, smiling at Ben:* Going in to brew it myself, honey.

She disappears into house. Marcus comes forward on the porch, sees Ben and Jake.

MARCUS, *stares at Jake:* Jake, take the boxes in. *Jake starts in.* And put Mr. Benjamin's valise out of your hand. *Jake hesitates, looks puzzled. Ben stares up at Marcus. Then Jake puts valise down, exits.* How was the world of fashion, Benjamin?

BEN: I was only in it for twenty-four hours.

MARCUS: Ah. That isn't long enough.

BEN: You ordered me back.

MARCUS: What for?

BEN, *looks up, smiles:* The pleasure of it, I think.

MARCUS, *giggles:* Certainly. But what did I call the pleasure?

BEN: You said the books needed checking, and I was to be back to do them today.

MARCUS, *thinks:* Books? I wouldn't let you touch the books in my library, Benjamin. Certainly you know that.

BEN, *annoyed:* Books for the store. *Store. Bookkeeping. Accounts.*

MARCUS: Oh. But why today?

BEN: I don't know, Papa. I'd like to have stayed in Mobile. I had some business—

MARCUS, *clucks:* But I brought you back on a Sunday to look at store books. Now why did I do that? I must have had some reason. I'll think of it later. *He looks down, realizes Ben isn't going to answer.* What business did you have, Ben?

BEN: I wanted to invest two thousand dollars in Birmingham Coal, Incorporated. It will bring fifty thousand some day. There's coal there, and they're sending down men from the North with money for it— But I couldn't raise it. And you wouldn't lend it to me.

MARCUS: That why you went? That foolish old scheme of yours? I had hoped you went to Mobile for a lady.

BEN: No, sir. I have no lady.

MARCUS: I believe you. But certainly you went to the concert last night?

BEN: No, I didn't. I told you: I was trying to borrow the two thousand you wouldn't let me have.

MARCUS: Well, you must hear a good concert before you die.

Lavinia and Coralee enter from kitchen door.

MARCUS, *starts into his room:* Carry in your own valise, son. It is not seemly for a man to load his goods on other men, black or white.

Ben looks up, half annoyed, half amused. He picks up his valise, starts toward door as Coralee appears, carrying breakfast tray. Lavinia follows her. Ben watches them as Coralee puts tray on table. Lavinia, knowing that Marcus is on the balcony, but not knowing whether she should speak to him, helps Coralee by aimlessly fussing about with the tray.

LAVINIA, *to Ben:* Morning, son.

BEN: Morning, Mama.

LAVINIA: Pleasant trip?

BEN: No, unsuccessful.

LAVINIA: That's good, I'm sure. I mean— Morning, Marcus.

MARCUS: Coralee. I'll be right down. Lavinia, send everybody else to the dining room for breakfast. Go on, Lavinia.

He disappears. Lavinia spills coffee.

CORALEE, *quickly:* All right, Miss Viney. No harm. Go on in and have your breakfast before there's trouble.

LAVINIA: I was only trying—

Lavinia goes into living room as Marcus comes downstairs carrying a book. He goes immediately to table. Coralee pours coffee.

MARCUS: Who is down for breakfast?

CORALEE: I don't know.

LAVINIA, *reappears in living-room doorway:* Oh, Marcus, Colonel Isham is calling. Can he come out?

MARCUS: If he is capable of walking.

Colonel Isham, a man of sixty-five, appears in the doorway.

MARCUS: Colonel Isham.

ISHAM: You will forgive this too early visit?

MARCUS: You're in town for church?

ISHAM: I've come to see you. I was asked to come to see you.

MARCUS: To talk about bad cotton?

ISHAM: No, sir. I don't mix with a man's Sunday breakfast, to talk about cotton. I come to talk about your son Oscar.

MARCUS: Then you will need coffee.

ISHAM: Thank you, no. Two nights ago—

MARCUS: People like you don't drink coffee with people like me?

ISHAM: I've had coffee. Now, Mr. Hubbard—

MARCUS: Then come again when you haven't had it.

There is a pause. Slowly Isham comes to the table. Marcus smiles, pours a cup of coffee, hands it to Isham, who takes it and sits down.

ISHAM: Thank you. I have come here for your sake, Mr. Hubbard. There is dangerous feeling up in my town this morning—

MARCUS: Colonel, I hate conversations for my sake. Sunday is my day of study. I don't wish to sound rude but please say quickly what you have come about.

ISHAM, *smiles:* Mr. Hubbard, I'm too old to frighten.

MARCUS, *smiles:* And I should be a daring man to try it. You, one of our great heroes. Commanding the first Alabama troops at—

ISHAM, *sharply:* I am not interested in talking to you about the War Between the States, or about your personal war on the people of this state— Now, please listen to me. Two nights ago Sam Taylor in Roseville was badly beaten up. Last night fourteen people identified the night riders as the Cross boys, from over the line, and your son Oscar.

MARCUS, *shouts into the house:* Benjamin. Rope Oscar and bring him out here immediately. I told you fifteen years ago you were damn fools to let Klansmen ride around, carrying guns—

ISHAM: Were you frightened of our riding on you? I came here to tell you to make your son quit. He can thank me he's not swinging from a rope this minute. You have good reason to know there's not a man in this county wouldn't like to swing up anybody called Hubbard. I stopped my friends last night but I may not be able to stop them again. Tell him what patriots do is our business. But he's got no right to be riding down on anybody—

Ben, followed by Oscar, appears in the dining-room doorway. Oscar looks frightened, decides to be cute.

OSCAR: *Rope* me out. I can stand up, Papa. Never felt my Saturday night liquor that bad—

ISHAM, *ignoring Oscar, to Marcus:* Taylor is a good

man. He's got no money for treatment, got no job now, won't get one again.

MARCUS, *to Oscar:* Colonel Isham has just saved you from a lynching party. Should I thank him?

OSCAR, *terrified:* Lynching! What did— Colonel Isham —I—

ISHAM: I don't want to speak with you.

MARCUS: Who does?

OSCAR: But what did I—

MARCUS: Do I have to tell you that if you ever put on those robes again, or take a gun to any man— *Takes roll of bills from his pocket, throws it to Benjamin:* Count out five hundred dollars, Benjamin.

OSCAR, *very nervous:* You mean Taylor? I wasn't riding with the Klan boys. No, I wasn't. I was thinking about it, but—

BEN: No, he couldn't have been with them. He took me to the Mobile train, and the train was late, so we sat talking. He couldn't have got up to Roseville.

ISHAM: You say you're willing to swear to that, Mr. Benjamin? You sure you're willing to go against fourteen people identifying your brother—?

BEN: Oh, Oscar looks like anybody.

MARCUS, *smiles:* Give the money to Colonel Isham, Benjamin. Go away, Oscar. *Oscar exits through dining-room door.* Please use the money for Taylor.

ISHAM: We'll take care of him, Hubbard. Good day, sir.

MARCUS: You won't take care of him, because you can't. Learn to be poor, Isham, it has more dignity. Tell Taylor there will be a check each month. Tell him that my other son, Benjamin, wishes to make amends. Ben has a most charitable nature.

Isham hesitates, decides, takes the money, looks at it.

ISHAM: There is no need for so much. A hundred would be more proper.

MARCUS: Good day, Colonel. Don't give me lectures on propriety.

Isham starts to speak, changes his mind, exits left toward street. There is a pause. Ben looks at Marcus, drops the roll of money on Marcus's table.

BEN, *smiles:* You didn't like my story about Oscar?

MARCUS: Not much. Very loyal of you, however.

BEN: I like it.

MARCUS: Good. It's yours. Keep it. You must have one of your usual involved reasons for wanting it.

BEN: Five hundred dollars is a lot of money to a man who allows himself six dollars for a trip to Mobile.

MARCUS: Perhaps you're stingy.

BEN: You can't be much else on a salary of twenty dollars a week.

MARCUS: Is that all I pay you? Ah, well, you'll be better off when I—if and when I die. But I may not die; did I tell you, Benjamin?

Regina, Oscar and Lavinia appear from the living room. Regina hurries to Marcus.

REGINA: Forgive me, darling. I forgot your coffee.

Oscar is carrying a cup of coffee and a roll. Lavinia, who never sees anything, bumps into him. Oscar turns on her angrily.

OSCAR: Goodness sake, Mama. Watch where you going.

REGINA: Oscar's in a bad humor this morning. Oscar's got one of those faces shows everything.

LAVINIA, *to everybody—nobody pays any attention:* I'm sorry. I'm sure I didn't mean to—

MARCUS: Oscar has good reason for being in a bad humor. He owes me five hundred dollars.

Oscar's hand begins to shake on the cup. He rattles the spoon and saucer.

BEN: For God's sake sit down and stop rattling that cup.

OSCAR: Papa, you can't mean that— Ben told you where I was. I wasn't even—

MARCUS, *to Regina:* You look charming. New?

REGINA: No. But I *did* buy a few new dresses.

MARCUS: A few? I saw the boxes coming in.

OSCAR: Seven dresses. Seven, I counted them.

REGINA: Can you count up to seven now? And more coming next week, Papa.

MARCUS: What are you going to do with them, honey?

REGINA, *hesitates, then gaily:* Could we go for a walk?

BEN: You buying these clothes out of your allowance?

REGINA, *laughs:* Aren't you silly? How could I? There's a fur piece and a muff that cost three hundred dollars alone. They're charming, Papa, wait till you see them—

OSCAR, *delighted at the diversion in the conversation:* You really gone crazy? Nobody's ever worn furs in this climate since old lady Somers put that bear rug around her and jumped out the porch.

REGINA: I won't jump out the porch.

BEN: I will have to O.K. the bills, so would you tell me how much you've spent?

REGINA, *airily:* I don't know. I didn't even ask.

OSCAR, *shrilly:* Didn't even ask? Didn't even ask? You gone real crazy, acting like Miss Vanderbilt, whatever her name is—rich people up North don't act that way. They watch their money, and their fathers' money.

REGINA: Oh, that's not true. Those people in Chicago, just the other day, gave their daughter a hundred-thousand-dollar check for a trousseau—

BEN, *looks at her:* A trousseau? So that's what you're buying? I saw Horace Giddens in Mobile last evening, and he was mighty disappointed you haven't answered his letter about coming up for another visit here.

OSCAR: Hey, he wouldn't be bad for you, Regina—

BEN: He's in love with you. That was obvious when he was here. It's good society, that family, and rich. Solid, quiet rich.

OSCAR: And you'd get to like him. A lot of people get married not liking each other. Then, after marriage, they still don't like each other much, I guess—

BEN, *sharply:* Are you still drunk?

LAVINIA, *comes to life:* A wedding? That would be nice. I hope you make your plans right quick, Regina, because—

MARCUS, *very slowly:* What is all this, Regina?

LAVINIA: I didn't say anything. I was twisting my handkerchief—

REGINA: It's nothing, Papa, nothing. You know Ben. You know he wants me to marry money for him. I'm not even thinking about Giddens. I don't like him.

BEN: Certainly I want you to marry money. More than that— *She wheels around to stare at him.* You're twenty years old. You ought to be settled down. You been worrying us. *Pleased at the nervousness Regina is showing:* Isn't that so, Mama? Hasn't Regina been worrying you?

LAVINIA: I really don't know, son. I really couldn't say.

OSCAR: Well, I could say she's been worrying me. Many's the time I thought of taking action. Sashaying around as open as—

REGINA, *to Oscar:* Oh, shut up. *To Marcus:* Papa. You can't blame me if Ben thinks up one of his plans to annoy you, and Oscar chimes in like he always does. I bought the clothes because I—because I want to take a little trip. That's all, Papa.

MARCUS: A trip?

REGINA: All right. I'll send back the dresses. I don't know what all this talk's about. *Comes to him:* Spoiling your Sunday. Come on, darling. Let's take our lunch and go on a picnic, just you and me. We haven't done that in a long time.

MARCUS: No, not for a long time. *To Ben:* Something amuses you?

BEN: Yes. You and Regina.

MARCUS, *to Ben and Oscar:* The two of you have contrived to give me a bad morning. *To Oscar:* And you have cost me five hundred dollars. How much you drawing at the store?

OSCAR, *nervous but determined:* I was going to talk to you about that, Papa. I'm drawing sixteen a week. It ain't enough, Papa, because, well, I'm getting on and I want a little life of my own. I was going to ask you if you couldn't sort of make a little advance against a little raise—

MARCUS: You'll get eleven a week hereafter. Five dollars will go to repay me for the five hundred.

OSCAR: My God, Papa. You can't— Eleven a week! My

God, Papa— That wasn't what I meant. You misunderstood me 'cause I wasn't talking clear. I wanted a little *raise,* not a—

MARCUS, *to Ben, sharply:* Put aside your plans for your sister's future. Spend with profit your time today going over the store books. *Then, amused:* You'll find we are short of cash. Call in some cotton loans or mortgages. *Giggles.* Then go to church.

LAVINIA, *delighted:* Want to come with me, Benjamin? I'm going to my church, because they're saying a prayer for my birthday. *To Marcus:* It's my birthday, Marcus.

MARCUS: Congratulations, Lavinia.

LAVINIA: Thank you. *Comes to Marcus:* We were going to talk today. You promised, Marcus—

MARCUS: I promised to talk? Talk about what?

LAVINIA, *amazed, worried:* Talk about what? You know, Marcus. You promised last year, on my last birthday. You said you were too busy that day, but this year you said—

MARCUS: I'm still busy, my dear. Now you run and tell Belle to make us up a fine picnic basket. *To Regina:* And a good bottle of wine. I'll get it myself.

LAVINIA: But, Marcus, I been waiting since last year—

MARCUS: Get the lunch now. *She hesitates, looks frightened, goes toward kitchen door. To Regina:* I'll bring my Aristotle. You'll read in English, I'll follow you in Greek. Shall we walk or drive?

REGINA, *smiling:* Let's walk. You get the wine and your books. I'll change my clothes— *He nods, smiles, goes into house. She stops to look at Ben, smiles:* You never going to learn, Ben. Been living with Papa for thirty-five years, and never going to learn.

OSCAR: Regina, you got a few hundred dollars to lend me? Wouldn't take me long to pay it back—

BEN: Learn what, honey?

OSCAR: Papa's sure hard on me. It's unnatural. If a stranger came in he'd think Papa didn't like me, his own son.

REGINA, *turns to Oscar:* You want some money? If you had any sense, you'd know how to get it: just tell Papa *Ben* don't want you to have it. You'll get it. *To Ben:* You ain't smart for a man who wants to get somewhere. You should have figured out long ago that Papa's going to do just whatever you tell him not to do, unless *I* tell him to do it. *Pats his shoulder.* Goodness gracious, that's been working for the whole twenty years I been on earth.

BEN, *to Regina:* You are right, and you're smart. You must give me a full lecture on Papa some day; tell me why he's so good to you, how you manage, and so on.

REGINA, *laughs:* I'm busy now, taking him on a picnic.

BEN: Oh, not now. Too hot for lectures. We'll wait for

a winter night. Before the fire. I'll sit opposite you and you'll talk and I'll listen. And I'll think many things, like how you used to be a beauty but at fifty years your face got worn and sour. Papa'll still be living, and he'll interrupt us, the way he does even now: he'll call from upstairs to have you come and put him to bed. And you'll get up to go, wondering how the years went by— *Sharply:* Because, as you say, he's most devoted to you, and he's going to keep you right here with him, all his long life.

REGINA, *angrily:* He's not going to keep me here. And don't you think he is. I'm going away. I'm going to Chicago— *Ben gets up, stares at her. Oscar looks up. She catches herself:* Oh, well, I guess you'd have to know. But I wanted him to promise before you began any interfering— I'm going for a trip, and a nice long trip. So you're wrong, honey.

BEN, *slowly:* He's consented to the trip?

REGINA, *giggles:* No. But he will by the time the picnic's over.

OSCAR: Chicago? You sure got Mama's blood. Little while now, and you're going to be just as crazy as Mama.

REGINA, *to Ben:* And the trip's going to cost a lot of money. I got books from hotels, and I know. But you'll be working hard in the store and sending it on to me—

BEN: You could always come home occasionally and go on another picnic. *Comes up to her:* This time I don't think so. Papa didn't just get mad about you and

Horace Giddens. Papa got mad about you and any man, or any place that ain't near him. I wouldn't like to be in the house, for example, the day he ever hears the gossip about you and Bagtry— *Sharply:* Or is Bagtry going to Chicago—

REGINA, *tensely, softly:* Be still, Ben.

OSCAR: And everybody sure is gossiping. Laurette even heard it up in Roseville. I said there's nothing between you. I wouldn't believe it. But if ever I thought there was I'd ride over to Lionnet, carrying a gun. I sure would—

REGINA, *carefully:* And the day you do I'll be right behind you. It'll be your last ride, darling.

OSCAR, *backing away:* All right, all right, I was joking. Everybody's talking so wild today—

REGINA, *turns back to Ben:* Look, Ben, don't start anything. I'll get you in trouble if you do.

BEN: I believe you.

REGINA: Wish me luck. I got a hard day's work ahead. *She goes up steps to upper porch and into her room.*

OSCAR, *yawns:* Where she going?

BEN: Try to keep awake. Why did you beat up Sam Taylor?

OSCAR, *after a second, sulkily:* He's a no-good carpetbagger.

BEN, *wearily:* All right. Let's try again. Why did you beat up Sam Taylor?

OSCAR: He tried to make evening appointments with Laurette. He tried it twice. I told him the first time, and I told her too.

BEN: Is Laurette the little whore you've been courting?

OSCAR, *slowly, tensely:* Take that back, Ben. Take back that word. *Ben laughs. Oscar advances toward him, very angry:* I don't let any man—

BEN: Now listen to me, you clown. You put away your gun and keep it away. If those fools in your Klan want to beat up niggers and carpetbaggers, you let 'em do it. But you're not going to make this county dangerous to me, or dangerous to the business. We had a hard enough time making them forget Papa made too much money out of the war, and I ain't ever been sure they forgot it.

OSCAR: Course they haven't forgot it. Every time anybody has two drinks, or you call up another loan, there's plenty of talk, and plenty of hints I don't understand. *Rises.* If I had been old enough to fight in the war, you just bet I'd been right there, and not like you, bought off. I'm a Southerner. And when I see an old carpetbagger or upstart nigger, why, I feel like taking revenge.

BEN: For what? Because Papa got rich on them? *Very sharply:* Put away that gun, sonny, and keep it put away, you hear me?

OSCAR, *frightened:* All right, all right. I want to thank

you. I forgot. For saying that I was talking to you on the train. Thanks, Ben.

BEN: I wasn't lying for you. I was trying to save five hundred dollars.

OSCAR, *hurt:* Oh. Guess I should have known. *Sighs:* How'm I ever going to pay it back? I'm in a mess. I— Ben, help me, will you? I'm deeply and sincerely in love.

BEN: Go give yourself a cooling sponge bath.

OSCAR: I want to marry Laurette. I was going to ask Papa to advance me a little money, so we could ship on down to New Orleans. He's going to leave money when he dies, plenty of it. I just want a little of mine now, and I'll go away—

BEN: He won't leave much. Not at this rate. He's spent forty thousand on nothing in the last six months.

OSCAR: My God, forty thousand and us slaving away in the store! And that's the way it's always going to be. I'm telling you: I'm taking Laurette and I'm going. Laurette's a fine girl. Hasn't looked at another man for a year.

BEN: Well, she better take them up again if you're going away. *You* can't earn a living.

Jake appears from the living room.

JAKE: Mr. Ben, a lady who says she doesn't want to say her name, she would like to speak with you. She's in the front hall, waiting.

BEN: Who? Who is it?

JAKE: Miss Birdie Bagtry.

Ben and Oscar turn in surprise.

BEN, *after a minute:* Wants to see *me?* *Jake nods vigorously.* Bring her out. *Jake exits.*

OSCAR: Now what do you think of that? What's she want to come here for? To see *you?* *Giggles.* What you been up to, boy?

BEN: Maybe she's come to look at you. Didn't you tell me she once gave you a glass of lemonade?

OSCAR: Did she?

BEN: I don't know. I only know that you told me so.

OSCAR: Then I guess it happened.

BEN: That doesn't necessarily follow.

OSCAR: Well, it was true. I was pushing a lame horse past Lionnet. I was lame myself from something or other—

BEN: Laurette Sincee?

OSCAR: I told you once, stop that. I am in love with Laurette, deeply and sincerely.

BEN: Better you'd stayed for the lemonade and fallen in love with Lionnet's cotton-fields.

OSCAR: Oh, this girl's supposed to be awfully silly. Melty-mush-silly. *Smiles:* That's what Laurette calls people like that. Melty-mush-silly.

BEN: She's witty, Laurette, eh? *Jake appears in the living-room door followed by a slight, pretty, faded-looking girl of twenty. Her clothes are seedy, her face is worn and frightened.* Good morning, ma'am.

OSCAR, *with charm:* Well, hello there, Miss Birdie!

BIRDIE, *bows:* Mr. Benjamin. And morning to you, Mr. Oscar. *Nervously:* We haven't seen you in many a long day. You haven't been hunting lately?

OSCAR: Oh, my time's been taken up with so many things, haven't had much chance.

BIRDIE *nods:* I know, you gentlemen in business. Please, you all, forgive my coming to your house, particularly on this day of privacy. I'll just take a few minutes and—

OSCAR: Excuse me, Miss Birdie. Hope you'll come again. *He starts toward room.*

BEN: Wait inside, Oscar. *Oscar turns to stare at him, then shrugs, disappears. To Birdie:* Please.

BIRDIE, *sits down:* Yes, sir. Thank you.

BEN: Can I get you coffee?

BIRDIE: No, sir. Thank you. You see, I only got a few minutes before Mama begins wondering. I'm sorry to worry you here, but I couldn't come to see you in the store, because then the whole town would know, wouldn't they? And my Mama and Cousin John would just about— *Giggles nervously.* Isn't that so, Mr. Benjamin?

BEN: Isn't what so?

BIRDIE, *very nervous:* About knowing. I must apologize for disturbing— Oh, I said that before. It's not good manners to take up all your time saying how sorry I am to take up all your time, now is it? *Giggles.* Oh, and I'm doing that again, too. Mama says I say everything in a question. Oh.

BEN: What do you want to talk to me about, Miss Birdie?

BIRDIE: Yes. *Rises. Desperately:* Mr. Benjamin, we're having a mighty bad time. It can't go on. It got so bad that last month Mama didn't want to do it, but she did it, and it was just awful for her.

BEN, *after a second, politely:* Did what?

BIRDIE: Went all the way to Natchez, just to keep from going to our kinfolk in Mobile. Course they're so poor now they couldn't have done anything anyway, but just to keep them from knowing she went all the way to Natchez.

BEN: Really?

BIRDIE: Yes, sir, all the way by herself. But they said they just couldn't. They said they'd like to, for Papa's dead sake and Grandpapa's, but they just couldn't. Mama said she didn't want it for anybody's sake, not like that, not for those reasons—well, you know Mama, Mr. Benjamin.

BEN: No, I don't.

BIRDIE: Oh. Well, I don't blame her, although . . . No, when everything else is gone, Mama says you at least got pride left. She did it to save me, Mr. Benjamin, the trip, I mean. I was such a ninny, being born when I did, and growing up in the wrong time. I'm much younger than my brothers. I mean I am younger, if they were living. But it didn't do any good.

BEN: I beg your pardon?

BIRDIE: The trip to Natchez. It didn't do any good.

BEN: What kind of good didn't it do? *She looks puzzled.* Why did your Mama make the trip?

BIRDIE: To borrow money on the cotton. Or on the land—*softly*—or even to sell the pictures, or the silver. But they said they couldn't: that everybody was raising cotton that nobody else wanted. I don't understand that. I thought people always wanted cotton.

BEN: They will again in fifty years.

BIRDIE, *after a pause:* Oh. Fifty years. *Smiles sadly.* Well, I guess we can't wait that long. The truth is, we can't pay or support our people, Mr. Benjamin, we can't— Well, it's just killing my Mama. And my Cousin John, he wants to go away.

BEN: Where does he want to go?

BIRDIE: Away from here. *Tense, very frightened:* Forgive me. Would you, I mean your father and you, would you lend money on our cotton, or land, or—

BEN: Your Cousin John, does he want to go to New York or Chicago, perhaps? Has he spoken of going to Chicago?

BIRDIE: Oh dear, no. There's no war going on in Chicago.

BEN: I beg your pardon?

BIRDIE: A war. He wants to go back to war. Mama says she can even understand that. She says there isn't any life for our boys any more.

BEN: I see. Where will Captain Bagtry find a war?

BIRDIE: There's something going on in Brazil, John says. He looked it up in the paper, and he's got a map.

BEN: Brazil. Is there a nice war going on in Brazil?

BIRDIE: Yes. I think so. *Eagerly:* You see, that was one of the things Mama was going to do with the money. Pay all our people and give John the carfare. He can earn a lot in Brazil, he can be a general. *Pauses, breathes:* Now about the loan, Mr. Benjamin—

BEN: You will inherit Lionnet?

BIRDIE: Me? Er. Yes. You mean if Mama were to— You mustn't believe those old stories. Mama's not so sick that a little good care and— *Very embarrassed:* I'm sorry.

BEN: You don't want your Mama to know you've come here?

BIRDIE: Oh, no, no. She'd never forgive me, rather die—

BEN, *laughs:* To think you had come to us.

BIRDIE: I didn't mean that. I am so sorry. I didn't—

BEN: You have not offended me, ma'am. I only ask because as I understand it you don't own Lionnet, your Mama does. But you don't want her to know about the loan. And so who would sign for it?

BIRDIE, *stares at him:* I would. Oh. You mean you can't sign for what you don't own. Oh. I see. I hadn't thought of that. Oh. That's how much of a ninny I am. Forgive me for bothering you. I shouldn't have. I'm sorry I just ruined your Sunday morning. Good day, sir.

BEN, *goes to dining-room door:* Oscar, Oscar, I know you want to walk Miss Bagtry home.

BIRDIE: Oh, no. Thank you. I—

OSCAR, *calling, offstage:* I have an appointment. I'm late.

BIRDIE, *embarrassed:* Please, sir—

BEN, *to Birdie:* How much of a loan were you thinking about?

BIRDIE: Five thousand dollars. It would take that much to pay our people and buy seed and pay debts and—But I guess I was as foolish about that as—

BEN: You know, of course, that all loans from our company are made by my father. I only work for him. Yours is good cotton and good land. But you don't own it. That makes it hard. It's very unusual, but perhaps I could think of some way to accommodate you. A promise from you, in a letter—

BIRDIE, *delighted:* Oh. Oh. Of course, I'd make the promise.

BEN: Why don't you talk to my father yourself? I'll tell him what it's all about, and you come back this afternoon—

BIRDIE, *backing away:* Oh, no. I couldn't say all that today again. I just couldn't— *Softly:* That's silly. Of course I could. What time will I come?

BEN: I have a pleasanter idea. Come tomorrow evening. Once a month my father has a music evening with musicians from Mobile to play on the violin, and flatter him. He's always in a good humor after his music. Come in then, Miss Birdie, and please invite Captain Bagtry to escort you.

BIRDIE: You really think there's any chance? Your Papa would— And my Mama wouldn't ever have to find out?

BEN, *bows:* I will do my best for you before you come.

BIRDIE, *after a second, with determination:* Thank you very much. I will be most pleased to come. Imagine having a concert right in your own house! I just love music. *Oscar appears in the door, stares angrily at Ben.* Thank you for your courtesy in offering to walk me back, Mr. Oscar. And thank you, Mr. Benjamin. *Birdie smiles happily, moves quickly off.*

OSCAR, *comes close to Ben, softly, very angry:* What the hell's the matter with you? Bossing me around, ruining my day?

BEN, *softly:* Be nice to the girl. You hear me?

OSCAR: I'm taking her home. That's enough. Damned little ninny.

BEN: I was thinking of trying to do you a favor. I was thinking if something works right for me, I'd lend you the five hundred to pay Papa back.

OSCAR: Squee, Ben! If you only could. What would you be doing it for?

BEN: Because I want you to be nice to this girl. Flatter her, talk nice. She's kind of pretty.

OSCAR: Pretty? I can't stand 'em like that.

BEN: I know. Virtue in woman offends you. Now go on. Be charming. Five hundred possible dollars' charming.

OSCAR, *smiles:* All right. *He runs off. After a minute Marcus, carrying three books and a bottle of wine, appears on the porch.*

MARCUS, *reading:* "The customary branches of education number four. Reading and writing." You know *those,* Benjamin, I think. "Gymnastic exercise"—*Marcus laughs*—"and music." Aristotle. *You* don't know any music, Benjamin.

BEN: I've been too busy, Papa.

MARCUS: At what?

BEN: Working all my life for you. Doing a lot of dirty jobs. And then watching you have a wild time throwing the money around. But when I ask you to lend me a little . . .

MARCUS: You're a free man, Benjamin. A free man. You don't like what I do, you don't stay with me. *Holding up the book:* I do wish you would read a little Aristotle, take your mind off money.

Regina comes down the steps, in a new dress, carrying a parasol and a steamer rug.

BEN, *looks at her:* Oh. Before I forget. I invited Miss Birdie Bagtry and her cousin to come here tomorrow night.

MARCUS: To come here? What do you mean?

BEN: I thought you'd like having the quality folk here. *Smiles:* Come here to beg a favor of you.

MARCUS, *stares at him, giggles:* You teasing me?

BEN: No. The girl just left here. She wants us to lend money on the cotton. Her Mama didn't know, and mustn't know. But Miss Birdie doesn't own the place—

MARCUS: Then what kind of nonsense is that?

BEN: Maybe it's not nonsense. Take a note from her. If she dies before her mother—

MARCUS, *sharply:* Who said anything about dying? You're very concerned with people dying, aren't you?

BEN, *laughs:* You hate that word. *Quickly:* Her mother could get out of it legally, maybe, but I don't think she would. Anyway, the old lady is sick, and it's worth a chance. Make it a short loan, call it in in a few years. They've wrecked the place and the money won't do 'em much good. I think the time would come when you'd own the plantation for almost nothing— *Looks up at Regina.* A loan would make them happy, and make us money. Make the Bagtrys grateful to us—

REGINA, *softly:* Course I don't know anything about business, Papa, but could I say something, please? I've been kind of lonely here with nobody nice having much to do with us. I'd sort of like to know people of my own age, a girl my own age, I mean—

MARCUS, *to Ben:* How much does she want?

BEN, *hesitates for a minute:* Ten thousand.

MARCUS: On Lionnet? Ten thousand is cheap. She's a fool.

BEN, *smiles:* Yes, I think she's a fool.

MARCUS, *giggles:* Well, the one thing I never doubted was your making a good business deal. Kind of cute of you to think of their coming here to get it, too. Bagtrys in this house, begging. Might be amusing for an hour.

REGINA, *quickly:* Can't invite 'em for an hour, Papa. And we've got to be nice to them. Otherwise I just wouldn't want to see him come unless we'd be awful nice and polite.

MARCUS: They'll think we're nice and polite for ten thousand.

REGINA, *laughs, in a high good humor:* I guess. But you be pleasant to them—

MARCUS: Why, Regina? Why are you so anxious?

REGINA: Papa, I told you. I been a little lonesome. No people my age ever coming here— I do think people like that sort of want to forgive you, and be nice to us—

MARCUS, *sharply, angrily:* Forgive me?

REGINA, *turns away, little-girl tearful:* I'm mighty sorry. What have I done? Just said I'd like to have a few people to listen to your old music. Is that so awful to want?

MARCUS, *quickly, pleadingly:* Come on, darling. *Shouts:* Lavinia, *where* is the basket? Lavinia! Coralee! *To Regina:* Come on now, honey. It's been a long time since you been willing to spend a Sunday with me. If I was sharp, I'm sorry. Don't you worry. I'll be charming to the visiting gentry.

BEN: Miss Birdie got a fear of asking you for the loan and of her cousin, John, knowing about it. Might be better if you just gave your consent, Papa, and didn't make her tell the story all over again. I can do the details.

Lavinia appears with a basket. Marcus takes it from her, peers in it.

MARCUS, *to Regina:* That's mighty nice-looking. We'll have a good lunch. *To Ben:* I don't want to hear the woes of Lionnet and Mistress Birdie. Most certainly you will do the details. Be kind of pleasant owning Lionnet. It's a beautiful house. Very light in motive, very well conceived—

LAVINIA: You going now, Marcus? Marcus! You promised you'd talk to me. Today—

MARCUS: I'm talking to you, Lavinia.

LAVINIA: Last year this morning, you promised me it would be today—

MARCUS, *gently:* I'm going out now, Lavinia.

LAVINIA: I've fixed you a mighty nice lunch, Marcus, the way you like it. I boiled up some crabs right fast, and—

MARCUS: I'm sure. Thank you. *He starts to move off.*

LAVINIA, *comes running to him:* Please, Marcus, I won't take up five minutes. Or when you come back? When you come back, Marcus?

MARCUS: Another day, my dear.

LAVINIA: It can't be another day, Marcus. It was to be on my birthday, this year. When you sat right in that chair, and I brought my Bible and you swore—

MARCUS: Another day.

LAVINIA: It ought to be today. If you swear to a day, it's got to be that day— *Very frightened:* Tomorrow then. Tomorrow wouldn't hurt so much, because tomorrow is just after today— I've *got* to go this week, because I had a letter from the Reverend—

REGINA: Oh, Mama. Are you talking that way again?

LAVINIA, *shaking, wildly:* Tomorrow, Marcus? Tomorrow, tomorrow.

MARCUS, *to Ben:* Ben, get Coralee.

LAVINIA: Tomorrow— *Ben exits. She grabs Marcus's arm:* Promise me tomorrow, Marcus. Promise me. I'll go get my Bible and you promise me—

MARCUS, *very sharply:* Stop that nonsense. Get hold of yourself. I've had enough of that! I want no more.

LAVINIA, *crying:* I'm not making any trouble. You know that, Marcus. Just promise me tomorrow.

MARCUS: Stop it! I've had enough. Try to act like you're not crazy. Get yourself in hand. *He exits.*

REGINA, *as Coralee appears:* Never mind, Mama. Maybe you'll be coming away with me. Would you like that? There are lots of churches in Chicago—

CORALEE: All right, Miss Regina. Don't tease her now.

REGINA, *gaily, as she goes off:* I'm not teasing.

After a pause, Lavinia sits down.

LAVINIA: Now I'm going to pretend. You ready?

CORALEE, *as if this had happened a thousand times before:* All right.

LAVINIA: He didn't say any of those things. He said he would speak with me sure thing— *Her voice rises:* No man breaks a Bible promise, and you can't tell me they do. You know I got my correspondence with the Reverend. He wants me to come and I got my mission and my carfare. In his last letter, the Reverend said if I was coming I should come, or should write him and say I couldn't ever come. "Couldn't ever come—" Why did he write that?

CORALEE: I don't know.

LAVINIA: Your people are my people. I got to do a little humble service. I lived in sin these thirty-seven years, Coralee. *Rocks herself.* Such sin I couldn't even tell you.

CORALEE: You told me.

LAVINIA: Now I got to finish with the sin. Now I got to do my mission. And I'll be— I'll do it nice, you know I will. I'll gather the little black children round, and I'll teach them good things. I'll teach them how to read and write, and sing the music notes and—

CORALEE, *wearily:* Oh, Miss Viney. Maybe it's just as well. Maybe they'd be scared of a white teacher coming among them.

LAVINIA, *after a pause:* Scared of me?

CORALEE, *turns:* No, ma'am. You're right. News of you has gone ahead.

LAVINIA: Course they could have many a better teacher.

I know mighty little, but I'm going to try to remember better. *Quietly:* And the first thing I'm going to remember is to speak to Marcus tomorrow. Tomorrow. *Turns pleadingly to Coralee:* I was silly to speak today. And I did it wrong. Anyway, he didn't say I *couldn't* go, he just said— *Stops suddenly.* My goodness, it's such a little thing to want. Just to go back where you were born and help little colored children to grow up knowing how to read books and— *Giggles.* You'll be proud of me. I'll remember things to teach them. You remember things when you're happy. And I'm going to be happy. You get to be fifty-nine, you don't be happy then, well, you got to find it. I'm going to be a very happy, happy, happy, happy— I'm going, Coralee. *She suddenly stops, looks down in her lap.*

CORALEE: Nice and cool in your room. Want to lie down? *Lavinia doesn't answer.* Want to play a little on the piano? Nobody's inside. *No answer. She waits, then very gently:* All right, if you don't want to. I tell you what. Come on in the kitchen and rest yourself with us.

Lavinia gets up, Coralee takes her arm, they start out as

CURTAIN FALLS

Act Two

SCENE: *The living room of the Hubbard house. This is the room we have seen through the French doors of the first act, and now we are looking at the room as if we were standing in the French doors of the portico. A large bay window is center stage, leading to a porch that faces the first-act portico. Right stage is a door leading to the dining room. Left stage is an open arch leading to the entrance hall and main staircase. The furniture is from the previous owner but Marcus has cleared the room of the ornaments and the ornamented. Right stage is a round table and three chairs. Left stage is a sofa and chair. Right, upstage, is a desk. Left, upstage, is a piano. Right, upstage, is a long table. Center of the room, before the columns of the porch, are a table and chairs. The room is simpler, more severe, than many rooms of the 1880's. A Greek vase, glass-enclosed, stands on a pedestal; a Greek statue sits on the table; Greek battle scenes are hung on the walls.*

As the curtain rises, Ben and Oscar are sitting at table, stage right. They each have a glass of port and the port decanter is in front of them. Marcus, Penniman and

Jugger are standing at a music stand, looking down at a music score. Penniman is a tall, fattish man. Jugger looks like everybody. Penniman looks up from the score, hums, drains his glass, looks at the empty glass, and crosses to Ben and Oscar. Marcus is intent on the score.

PENNIMAN, *meaning the score:* Very interesting. Harmonically fresh, eh, Mr. Benjamin?

BEN: I know nothing of music.

JUGGER: Why do people always sound so proud when they announce they know nothing of music?

PENNIMAN, *quickly, as Oscar fills his glass:* A fine port, and a mighty good supper. I always look forward to our evening here. I tell my wife Mrs. Hubbard is a rare housekeeper.

BEN: You like good port, Mr. Penniman?

PENNIMAN: Yes, sir, and don't trust the man who don't.

Oscar goes off into gales of laughter. This pleases Mr. Penniman and he claps Oscar on the shoulder. Marcus looks up, annoyed, taps bow on music stand. Penniman and Oscar stop laughing, Penniman winks at Oscar, carries his glass back to music stand. Jake comes from the hall entrance carrying two chairs, a lamp, and passes through to porch. Lavinia hurries in from the dining room. Her hair is mussy, her dress spotted. She looks around the room, smiles at everybody. When nobody notices her, she crosses to Marcus, leans over to examine the score, nods at what she reads.

LAVINIA: Oh, it's nice, Marcus. Just as nice as anybody could have. It's going to be a cold collation. Is that all right?

MARCUS, *who is in a good humor:* Yes, certainly. What's that?

LAVINIA: A cold collation? That's what you call food when you have guests. A cold collation.

PENNIMAN, *looks toward the dining room, delighted:* More food? After that fine supper—

LAVINIA: This is a special night. Guests. Isn't that pleasant? My, we haven't had guests— I don't think I remember the last time we had guests—

MARCUS, *looks at her:* All right, Lavinia.

LAVINIA: There'll be a dish of crabs, of course. And a dish of crawfish boiled in white wine, the way Belle does. And a chicken salad, and a fine strong ham we've been saving. *Stops.* Oh. I'm worrying you gentlemen—

PENNIMAN, *lifting his glass:* Worrying us? You, the honor of Rose County, and the redeemer of this family—

Jugger and Marcus look up sharply. Ben laughs. Marcus reaches over and takes Penniman's glass, carries it to table.

MARCUS: I am awaiting your opinion.

PENNIMAN, *who has the quick dignity of a man with too much port:* The judgment of music, like the inspiration for it, must come slow and measured, if it comes with truth.

OSCAR, *to Ben:* Talks like a Christmas tree, don't he?

LAVINIA: It's your third composition, isn't it, Marcus? Oh, I'm sure it's lovely. Just lovely.

MARCUS, *looks at her—softly:* How would you know, Lavinia?

LAVINIA, *hurt:* I can read notes, Marcus. Why, I taught you how to read music. Don't you remember, Marcus? *She goes toward Ben and Oscar.* I did. Yes, I did.

BEN, *amused:* Of course you did.

PENNIMAN, *hurriedly:* I would say this: It is done as the Greeks might have imposed the violin upon the lute. *Hums.* Right here. Close to Buxtehude— *Inspiration:* Or, the Netherland Contrapuntalists. Excellent.

Oscar pours himself another port, Lavinia has wandered to the piano, mumbling to herself.

MARCUS, *very pleased, to Penniman:* You like it?

PENNIMAN: I like it very much. And if you would allow us, I would like to introduce it in Mobile during the season. Play it first at the school, say, then, *possibly*—

MARCUS: That would make me very happy. And what do you think of it, Mr. Jugger?

JUGGER, *slowly:* Penniman speaks for me. He always does.

PENNIMAN, *quickly:* Come. We'll try it for you. I am

most anxious to hear it. *Points to Marcus's violin, coyly:* I daresay you know the solo part you have written for yourself?

MARCUS: Well, I—yes. *Very pleased:* I had hoped you would want to try it tonight. I— *Jugger picks up his violin, starts for portico. Marcus turns to him:* Mr. Jugger. Would *you* like to try it now?

JUGGER, *turns, looks at Marcus, seems about to say something, changes his mind:* I would like to try.

PENNIMAN: But where *is* my cello? Goodness God—

JUGGER, *sharply, at door of portico:* It's out here. When will you learn that it's hard to mislay a cello? *Penniman giggles, trips out to porch.*

LAVINIA, *suddenly plays a few notes on the piano:* See? I told you, Marcus. *That's* it. I told you I could read music just as good as I used to—

MARCUS: Is there something disturbing you this evening, Lavinia? More than usual?

Regina enters from the hall. She is dressed up, very handsome. They all turn to stare at her. She smiles, goes to Marcus.

MARCUS, *softly:* You're a beautiful girl.

OSCAR: Looks like the decorated pig at the county fair.

REGINA, *wheels around for Marcus:* It's my Chicago dress. *One* of my Chicago dresses. *Regina notices Lavinia:* Oh, Mama, it's late. Do go and get dressed.

LAVINIA: I'm dressed, Regina.

REGINA: You can't look like that. Put on a nice silk--

LAVINIA: I only have what I have—

REGINA: Put on your nice dress, Mama. It will do for tonight. We must order you new things. You can't go to Chicago looking like a tired old country lady—

LAVINIA, *wheels around:* *Chicago?* I'm not going to Chicago. Where I'm going I don't need clothes or things of the world. I'm going to the poor, and it wouldn't be proper to parade in silk— Marcus! You tell Regina where I'm going. *Tell her where I'm going.* You tell her right now. You—

REGINA: All right, Mama. Now don't you fret. Go upstairs and get dressed up for the high-toned guests. *She leads Lavinia to the hall.* Don't you worry now. Go on up, honey. Coralee's waiting for you. *She comes back into room. To Marcus:* Whew! I'm sorry. I should have known. I hope she isn't going to act queer the rest of the evening.

MARCUS: There's always that chance.

REGINA: Well, don't let's worry. *Gaily:* I'll see to everything. I'd better have a look in the kitchen, and more chairs— Let's have the very good champagne, Papa?

PENNIMAN, *from portico:* Mr. Hubbard—

MARCUS, *takes keys from his pocket, throws them to Ben:* Wine as good as Regina's dress. And count the bottles used. I don't want to find that Oscar has sold them again.

BEN, *to Regina:* So your picnic was successful? When do you leave for Chicago?

REGINA, *gaily:* In ten days, two weeks. *Comes to him.* Going to miss me?

BEN: Yes. Very much.

MARCUS: What's the matter? What's the matter, Regina?

REGINA, *gaily, leaving Ben:* Matter? Nothing. *Calls into dining room as she exits:* Two more chairs, Jake—

OSCAR: Now just tell me how I'm going to get word to Laurette that I can't meet her till later tonight, just somebody tell me that.

MARCUS, *very sharply to Ben:* I told you to get the wine.

Ben looks at him, smiles as if he understood why Marcus was angry, exits through dining-room door. Marcus stands staring at him. Then goes to piano, looks through scores. Oscar moves nervously toward Marcus.

OSCAR, *desperately:* Papa, I'm in trouble. You see, I had an appointment with a lady from out of town, Roseville, I mean.

MARCUS: What were they doing?

OSCAR: Who?

MARCUS: Regina and Ben when they were standing together— *Breaks off, turns sharply away.*

OSCAR: Oh, you know Ben. Always up to something. Yesterday, trying to marry off Regina, tonight trying to press me on the Bagtry girl.

MARCUS, *looks up:* Oh, come. Ben's not a fool. You and a Bagtry is a very comic idea.

OSCAR: I know, but Ben's figured they're so hard up for money they might even have me. It all fits in with this mortgage you're giving them, or something. He's got his eye on the cotton— *Giggles.* And Ben's eye goes in a lot of directions, mostly around corners. It's true, Papa. He made me take the girl home yesterday—

MARCUS, *looks at Oscar:* The mortgage, and then the girl and you. Interesting man, Benjamin.

OSCAR, *pleadingly:* Papa, like I say. I've got a friend who's waiting for me right now. I want you to meet her. You see, I'm deeply and sincerely in love. Deeply and sincerely. She's a fine girl. But *Ben* cries her down. *Ben* don't want me to be happy.

MARCUS: Isn't that too bad. Your own brother. It's a shame.

OSCAR: Course she's of the lower classes, and that doesn't fit in with Ben's plans for us to marry money for him. But the lower classes don't matter to me; I always say it's not how people were born but what they are—

MARCUS: You always say that, eh? Well, some people are democrats by choice, and some by necessity. You, by necessity.

OSCAR: Could I go fetch her here—*Desperately:* tonight? Could I, Papa?

MARCUS: What is this, a night at the circus?

OSCAR, *slyly, as a last chance:* I think it would just about finish Mr. Ben to have a member of the lower classes, sort of, mixing with the gentry, here. I thought it would sort of, sort of amuse you, and well, you could meet her at the same time. Be a good joke on Ben, sort of—

MARCUS, *slowly:* Is this Laurette that, that little, er—little thing from Roseville you been steaming about?

OSCAR: She's not, Papa. Oh, maybe she was a little wild before I met her, but— She was left an orphan and she didn't know what else to do, starving and cold, friendless.

MARCUS, *shudders:* Oh God, shut up. *Hesitates, then laughs.* All right, go and get her, if you like. Er. Does she come dressed? I wouldn't like her here, er, unrobed.

OSCAR, *hurt but happy:* Aw, she's a fine woman, Papa, don't talk like that. And she loves music. She wants to learn just about everything—

MARCUS: Don't bring her as a student, Oscar.

OSCAR: Oh, no. No, I wouldn't. She won't say a word. She admires you, Papa—

MARCUS: For what?

OSCAR: Well, just about, well, just for everything, I guess— *Marcus makes a dismissive gesture, goes on porch as Regina comes into room. Oscar sees Regina, smiles.* I'll be back in a few minutes. Going across the square to get Laurette, bring her here.

REGINA, *starts toward him, as Ben comes in carrying champagne bottles:* Here? That girl?—What's the matter with you? You're doing nothing of the kind. Come back here. You can't bring that—

OSCAR: Can't I? Well, just ask Papa. *He* wants her to meet my folks.

REGINA, *turns to Ben:* Ben, stop him. He can't bring her here tonight— Stop him! *But Oscar has disappeared:* Get him, Ben!

BEN: What am I supposed to do, shoot him? I'm too old to run down streets after men in love.

REGINA: He *can't* bring her here. You know what John will think. I saw him this afternoon: I had to beg him to come tonight. He doesn't know why Birdie wants him to come, but— Ben, he'll think we meant to do it, planned to insult them—

BEN: Yes, I'm sure he will.

The music on the porch begins.

REGINA: What's the matter with Papa? Why did he let Oscar—

BEN, *smiles: You're* going to learn some day about Papa. It's not as easy as you think, Regina. *They stand looking out to the porch, listening to the music.* He gave those clowns five thousand last month for something they call their music school. Now that they are playing his composition he should be good for another five thousand—

REGINA, *turns, softly, amazed:* Did he? Really? *Shakes her head:* Well, anyway, he's promised me plenty for—

BEN: To marry Bagtry? Enough to support you the rest of your life, you and your husband? I'm taking a vacation the day he finds out about your marriage plans.

REGINA, *angrily, nervous:* I don't know what you're talking about. Marry— What are you saying—? I— *Turns to him, tensely:* Leave me alone, Ben. Leave me alone. Stop making trouble. If you dare say *anything* to Papa about John, I'll—

BEN, *very sharply:* Don't threaten me. I'm sick of threats.

REGINA, *angry:* You'll be much sicker of them if you— *Then, softly:* Ben, don't. I'm in love with John.

BEN, *softly:* But he's not in love with you.

Lavinia comes into room, followed by Coralee who is pulling at her, trying to button her dress. Regina turns away from Ben.

LAVINIA: Don't bother with the lower buttons. *Timidly:* Am I proper now, daughter? *Regina doesn't answer her. Lavinia points out to porch, meaning the music.* You know, I've made myself cheer up. I know you were just teasing about Chicago, Regina, and I know full well

I've never been good about teasing. What do people do now, curtsy or shake hands? I guess it's just about the first guests we had since the suspicion on your Papa.

REGINA: Now, Mama. Please don't talk about any of that tonight. Don't talk at all about the war, or anything that happened. Please remember, Mama. Do you hear?

CORALEE, *quickly:* She won't. You all have been teasing her, and she's tired.

Coralee goes to Ben, takes the champagne bottles from the table. Jake comes in from the dining room carrying a tray of glasses and a punch bowl.

LAVINIA: Could I try the nice punch, Coralee?

CORALEE: You certainly can. *Jake exits. Ben starts to the table. As if such courtesy were unusual, Coralee stares at him:* Thank you, Mr. Ben.

Coralee exits. Ben pours three glasses of punch.

LAVINIA: Regina, when you don't frown you look like my Grandmama—*as Ben brings her a glass of punch, and moves on to Regina*—the one who taught me to read and write. And 'twas mighty unusual, a lady to know how to read and write, up in the piney woods.

BEN, *laughs:* Now, that's a safer subject, Mama. Tell the Bagtrys about our kinfolk in the piney woods. *He lifts his glass to Regina.* To you, honey.

REGINA, *smiles:* And to you, *honey.*

On the porch the music comes to an end. Regina who

has not, of course, been paying any attention, starts to applaud. She turns to Lavinia, indicates Marcus on porch.

LAVINIA: But I didn't hear it. I wasn't paying any attention.

Marcus comes into room.

REGINA, *goes to him:* It's brilliant of you, Papa.

MARCUS: I'm glad you liked it. Come along. We're about to start—*laughs*—the better-known classics.

BEN: Won't you wait for our guests?

MARCUS: Certainly not. I resent their thinking they can stroll in late on my music.

REGINA, *placatingly:* You're right, darling. *We'll* come out.

Marcus goes to porch. Regina follows. Ben follows her. Lavinia puts down her glass, follows Ben. Regina and Ben sit down, Lavinia sits down. The musicians tune up. Marcus, Penniman, and Jugger begin to play a divertimento by Leopold Mozart, a trio for violin, viola, and cello. Then the hall door opens and closes. On the porch, Regina and Ben both turn, turn back again. After a second, Oscar appears in the living room pulling Laurette Sincee. Laurette is about twenty, pig-face cute, a little too fashionably dressed. She stands in the door, admiring the room.

LAURETTE: Squee!

OSCAR, *proud and excited:* Not bad, eh? *Looks toward portico.* We got to talk soft.

LAURETTE: This *is* nice. You born here, Oskie?

OSCAR: No. Like I told you. Right after the war Papa bought—*giggles*—or something, this house from old man Reed. Like it?

LAURETTE: Squee. Who wouldn't?

OSCAR: Well, maybe, some day—

LAURETTE: Ah, go on, Oskie. Go on.

OSCAR: You just wait and see.

LAURETTE, *points to portico:* What's that?

OSCAR: What?

LAURETTE: The noise?

OSCAR: That's music, honey.

LAURETTE: Oh.

OSCAR: When you speak to Papa, tell him how much you like music. Tell him how fine he plays.

LAURETTE: What's he playing?

OSCAR: The violin.

LAURETTE: Ain't that a coincidence? I had a beau who said he played the violin. A Frenchman, much older than me. Had to leave his very own country because of the revolution.

OSCAR, *winces:* I don't like to hear about him, Laurette, him or any other men. I am deeply and sincerely in love with you.

LAURETTE, *pleasantly, but without too much interest:* Are you really, Oskie?

OSCAR: Laurette, I'm going to ask Papa for a loan. Then we'll go on down to New Orleans. Would you, Laurette—

LAURETTE: You've asked me the same question for the last year, twenty times. But you never yet asked your Papa for the loan.

OSCAR: I've been waiting for the right opportunity. I want you to be my *wife,* honey. I am deeply and—

LAURETTE: We can't eat on deeply and sincerely.

OSCAR: No, I know. But this is the big night, don't you see? *Laughs happily.* I never thought he'd let you come here. I mean—I mean a chance like this. And he's in a good humor about something. Now, darling, be very very—well, er. I tell you: you speak with him about what *he* likes. Tell him how much you think of music, not new music, mind you, but—and tell him how you stay awake reading.

LAURETTE: I've always been a reader. But I can't talk about it. What's there to say?

OSCAR: And he's fond of Mozart. Talk about Mozart.

LAURETTE: I can't do that.

OSCAR: Well, just try to please him. So much depends on it. We could have our own little place in New Orleans—

LAURETTE: What kind of place?

OSCAR: I'd find a job. You bet I would, and with you behind me to encourage and love me, with you to fight for, I'd forge ahead.

LAURETTE, *looks at him, puzzled:* Oh. Well, I'd certainly like to go to New Orleans. I know a girl there. She has an embroidery shop on Royal Street. I'm good at embroidery. It's what I always wanted to do. Did I ever tell you that? Always wanted to do embroidery.

OSCAR: Did you?

LAURETTE: Yep. Instead of whoring. I just wanted to do fancy embroidery.

OSCAR, *loudly, in a hurt cry:* Don't, Laurette, don't talk that way! *Ben and Regina, on the porch, look into room. Regina coughs loudly.* We better go out now.

LAURETTE: Why did your papa let me come tonight?

OSCAR: Don't let him worry you, honey. Just take it nice and easy. Pretend nobody knows anything about you, pretend you're just as good as them—

LAURETTE, *stares at him: Pretend?* Pretend I'm as good as anybody called Hubbard? Why, my Pa died at Vicksburg. He didn't stay home bleeding the whole state of Alabama with money tricks, and suspected of worse. You think I been worried for that reason?

OSCAR, *desperately:* No, no. I— For God's sake don't talk like that—

LAURETTE: You may be the rich of this county, but everybody knows how. Why, the Frenchman, I used to eat dinner with, and his sister, the Countess. What you mean, boy, your folks—?

OSCAR: I didn't mean anything bad. Haven't I just said I wanted to *marry* you? I think you're better than anybody.

LAURETTE: I'm not better than anybody, but I'm as good as piney wood crooks.

OSCAR, *puts his hand over her mouth, looks toward porch:* Stop, *please.* We've got to go outside. *Please—*

LAURETTE, *good-natured again:* Sometimes you bring out the worst in my nature, Oskie, and make me talk foolish. Squee, it's the truth—I am a little twitchy about coming here and meeting your folks. That's why I'm talking so brave. I ain't been in a place like this before. . . . *Pats him:* All right, I'll be very good and nice. I would like to go to New Orleans.

Oscar takes her in his arms. The front bell rings, but they don't hear it.

OSCAR: Course you would, with me. You love me, honey? *He leans down to kiss her.* Tell me you love me.

LAURETTE: Now, Oskie, you know this ain't the place or the time for mush—

Ben rises at the sound of the bell. As Ben comes from the porch, Jake brings in the Bagtrys. As they enter, Oscar is kissing Laurette, she is giggling, trying to push him away. The Bagtrys stop in the doorway as they see the scene. Ben comes to meet them, crosses stage. As he passes Oscar and Laurette, he shoves Oscar.

BEN: Excuse me. *As Laurette jumps away, Regina comes in from porch, tapping Lavinia on the arm as she comes. Ben speaks to Birdie:* My apologies. We don't always arrange this scene for our guests.

Birdie smiles nervously. John stares at Laurette.

OSCAR: We were just, I was, we were—

REGINA, *sharply:* All right. *Goes quickly to Birdie:* I am happy to have you here, Miss Birdie.

Birdie curtsies, puts out her hand, smiles warmly. Lavinia enters room.

JOHN, *bows to Regina, Ben, Oscar, then speaks to Laurette:* Hello, Laurette.

LAURETTE: Hello, John.

JOHN, *turns to Birdie:* Birdie, this is Miss Sincee.

LAURETTE: Finely, thank you.

Birdie bows.

LAVINIA, *hears Laurette speak and so hurries to her:* An honor to have you here, Miss Birdie—

REGINA, *sharply:* *This* is Miss Birdie, Mama.

LAVINIA, *who is shaking hands with Laurette, looks bewildered:* Oh. Sorry. I—

Oscar bumps into Lavinia, who is coming toward Birdie.

BIRDIE: I'm sorry we're late. I just couldn't seem to get dressed—

REGINA: Do come out now for the music.

They move out together. Lavinia speaks to Birdie.

LAVINIA: Come, ma'am. And you, Miss— *Brightly, to Birdie:* Is the other lady your sister?

LAURETTE, *annoyed, shoves Oscar:* What's the matter with you?

OSCAR: Oh. Mama, this is Miss Laurette Sincee. She's a visitor in town.

LAVINIA: Who's she visiting?

BEN: Us.

Ben reaches the porch door, stands aside to let Lavinia pass him. She looks puzzled, passes on to porch. Laurette, Oscar, Regina, John, are now seated on the porch. Lavinia sits near them. Birdie and Ben stand for a minute listening to the music.

BIRDIE: Nice. To have a special night, just to play music— I've heard your father is a very cultured gentleman. Have you been able, did he, speak of the matter that I—

BEN: Yes. We will make the loan.

BIRDIE, *turns radiant—softly:* Oh, what fine news! You can't imagine how worried I've been. I am very grateful to you, sir—

BEN: You don't have to be. It is a good loan for Hubbard Company, or my father wouldn't be taking it. We'll meet tomorrow, you and I, and work out the details.

BIRDIE: Oh, you won't have any trouble with me, Mr. Ben.

BEN: You wanted five thousand dollars, Miss Birdie. I have asked my father to lend you ten thousand.

BIRDIE, *puzzled—worried:* Oh. Mr. Ben, I don't need—

BEN, *quickly:* You can take five now, but if you should happen to need more, it will be there for you.

BIRDIE: But I won't need ten thousand dollars. No, indeed I won't. It's very kind of you, but—

BEN, *carefully:* You will only get five. I will keep the rest waiting for you. That's the way these things are done—*smiles*—sometimes.

BIRDIE: But it's bad enough to owe five thousand, not less ten—

BEN: *You will only owe five.* Now don't worry about it. Will you take my advice now about something else? Don't speak to my father about the loan. It is all arranged. And he's a man of such culture, as you say, that talk of money would disturb him on his music night.

BIRDIE, *gently:* Oh, of course. After all, it's a party, and as worried and pushing as I am, I wouldn't ever have talked business with him at a party.

BEN, *smiles down at her:* Good breeding is very useful. Thank you, Miss Birdie.

BIRDIE, *gently:* No, sir. It is I who must thank you.

He bows, stands aside, indicates porch. She moves to it, sits down. Ben stands in the doorway. The music continues. After a minute we see Oscar trying to move into the room. He leans over, bends down, moves rapidly into room, passes Ben. Laurette turns and Oscar beckons to her to come into room.

OSCAR: Papa going to play all night? *Crosses to get a drink.* Laurette's getting restless, sitting there.

BEN: She's not accustomed to a sitting position? Have another drink. I got a feeling you're going to need it.

LAURETTE, *enters the room from the porch:* Squce. I don't like this punch. It don't mean anything.

BEN: Can I put in a little brandy? I think that would make it mean more.

Marcus appears on the porch, comes up the aisle of chairs. He bows to Birdie and to John, comes into room. Oscar rushes to get him a drink of punch.

OSCAR: Papa, this is Miss Sincee.

MARCUS, *finishes drink, hands glass to Oscar:* How do you do?

LAURETTE: Finely, thank you. *Marcus stares at her. She becomes very nervous.* I love music, Mr. Hubbard. I had an uncle who played. *He* taught me to love music.

OSCAR, *too brightly:* Did he play the violin, like Papa?

LAURETTE: Er. Er. No. He had a little drum.

OSCAR, *very fast:* He liked Mozart. You told me, remember?

LAURETTE: Yeah. Sure did.

Regina and Birdie, followed by John and Lavinia, come in from the porch.

MARCUS: Miss Sincee pleases me. Her uncle played Mozart on a little drum. Have you ever heard of that, Miss Bagtry?

BIRDIE: Oh. Well, *I* haven't, but I'm sure there must be such an arrangement.

MARCUS, *looks at her with interest:* That's very kind of you, to be so sure. Do you play any instrument, Miss Bagtry? Not the little drum?

BIRDIE: Yes, sir. Not well. The piano.

MARCUS: Then you would oblige me—*she smiles, moves toward the piano, quickly*—some other night, very soon.

BIRDIE, *very flustered:* Yes. Yes, sir.

OSCAR: It's a coincidence, ain't it, that Laurette's Papa liked Mozart?

REGINA, *to Laurette:* I thought it was your uncle? Was your Papa the same as your uncle?

LAURETTE: What do you mean? Do you mean mon père was on one side of my family, and mon oncle on the other? I can understand *that.*

BEN, *fills her glass from the brandy decanter:* Your family were French?

LAURETTE: No. I learned that from a French gentleman who came from France. I don't know where he is now. I liked him.

BEN: Perhaps we could locate him for you.

LAURETTE: No. He married money.

REGINA: Oh, dear. All foreigners do, I guess. Light wines and light money.

LAURETTE: I never blamed him. I figured, well— *Looks at Regina:* You've had some bad experiences with Frenchmen?

Regina, Ben, and Marcus laugh.

BIRDIE, *to Marcus—making conversation:* John's been to Europe, you know.

MARCUS: I didn't know.

BIRDIE: Yes, he was. Just a few months before the war. Paris, France; London, England; St. Petersburg, Russia; Florence, Italy; Lake Como, Switzerland—

MARCUS: Your geography is remarkable.

BIRDIE: Oh, I only know because John kept a book. Pictures and notes and menus—if the war hadn't come, and my Papa had lived, I would have gone to Europe. It was planned for me to study water color.

MARCUS: Water color?

BIRDIE: Small water color. I like small water color.

MARCUS: Is that very different from large water color?

LAURETTE, *belligerently:* She means she likes small water color. What's the matter with that?

BIRDIE, *smiles at her:* Yes. *To Marcus:* You've been to Europe, Mr. Hubbard?

MARCUS, *laughs:* No, but I'm going. Might even settle down there. Yes, Regina?

REGINA, *looks at John, nervously:* Maybe some day, Papa. Chicago first.

MARCUS: Of course, we'll take our residence in Greece, but some place gayer, for Regina, at first. Perhaps you'd advise us, Captain Bagtry?

JOHN: I'd like to, sir. But I have no memory of Europe.

MARCUS, *turns elaborately in his chair:* Something unpleasant took it from your mind?

JOHN: No, sir. I just don't remember. It's as if I had never been there.

LAVINIA: I used to have a good memory. *Quickly:* I still have. Most of the time.

MARCUS, *very politely, to John:* Captain Bagtry, does anything stay in your memory, anything at all?

JOHN, *looks at Marcus, but the tone has been polite:* The war.

REGINA, *softly:* Only the war?

LAVINIA, *to John, motherly:* Well, I just bet. That's natural: you rode off so young.

JOHN, *turns to her:* Yes, ma'am. I can't remember the years before, and the years after have just passed like a wasted day. But the morning I rode off, and for three years, three months, and eight days after, well, I guess I remember every soldier, every gun, every meal, even every dream I had at night—

Ben is pouring Laurette another drink. Oscar is trying to keep her from having it. She pushes Oscar's hand.

LAURETTE: I wouldn't ever name a boy Oscar. It's silly.

REGINA: Well?

Marcus and Ben laugh. The others look embarrassed. Oscar makes an angry move, decides not to speak.

LAVINIA: I can't remember why we chose the name. Can you, Marcus?

MARCUS, *to Lavinia:* Your father's name was Oscar.

LAVINIA, *worried, crushed:* Oh, goodness, yes.

BIRDIE, *embarrassed, speaks quickly:* John's just wonderful about the war, Mr. Hubbard. Just as good as having a history book. He was everywhere: Vicksburg, Chattanooga, Atlanta.

MARCUS: And he remembers it *all?* What now seems to you the most important of your battles, Captain Bagtry?

JOHN, *annoyed:* I don't know. But there's no need for us to talk about the war, sir.

MARCUS: Oh, I'm interested. I know more of the Greek wars than I do of our own.

LAURETTE: Bet you anything there's a good reason for that. There's a good reason for everything in this vale of tears.

Marcus turns to stare at her.

BIRDIE: John, Mr. Hubbard says he's interested. Bet he'd like to hear about Vicksburg, just the way you always tell it to Mama and me.

Jake appears at the door.

JAKE: Supper's laid out, waiting.

MARCUS, *to John:* People remember what made them happy, and you were happy in the war, weren't you?

JOHN: Yes, sir. I was happy. I thought we would win.

MARCUS: I never did. Never, from the first foolish talk to the last foolish day. *John sharply turns away.* I have disturbed you. I'm most sorry. I speak the truth—whenever I can.

BIRDIE, *hastily:* Oh, John doesn't mind. He means—well, you see, it's hard for us to understand anybody who thought we'd lose—

JOHN, *sharply:* It's still hard for a soldier to understand.

BIRDIE, *quickly:* John means once a soldier, always a soldier. He wants to go to Brazil right now. Of course you know, Mr. Hubbard, the radical people down there are trying to abolish slavery, and ruin the country. John wants to fight for his ideals.

MARCUS: Why don't you choose the other side? Every man needs to win once in his life.

JOHN, *angrily:* I don't like that way of saying it. I don't necessarily fight for slavery, I fight for a way of life.

MARCUS: Supper, Captain. *Turns, calls to the porch:* Put away the music, gentlemen, and have a little more to eat. *Turns back to Regina:* What is disturbing you, Regina?

Lavinia, Birdie, Oscar, and Laurette exit to dining room.

REGINA, *sharply:* Nothing.

Ben exits.

MARCUS, *looks at John:* You disapprove of me, Captain?

JOHN: I am in your house, sir, and you forced me into this kind of talk.

Penniman and Jugger come through the room, go into the dining room.

MARCUS: Well, I disapprove of you. Your people deserved to lose their war and their world. It was a backward world, getting in the way of history. Appalling that you still don't realize it. Really, people should read more books.

REGINA, *angrily:* Papa, I didn't ask John here to listen to you lecture and be nasty and insulting.

MARCUS: *You* asked him here? You asked *John? Sharply:* Come in to supper, Regina.

REGINA, *very sharply:* When I'm ready, Papa. *Marcus*

looks at her, hesitates for a second, then goes into dining room. There is a pause. She goes to John: I am so sorry.

JOHN: Why should you be sorry? It's the way you feel, too.

REGINA, *impatiently:* All that damn war nonsense— Don't worry about Papa. I'll take care of him. You didn't give me a chance to tell you about Chicago—

JOHN: You didn't give me a chance to tell you about Brazil.

REGINA: Will you stop that foolish joke—

JOHN: It may not be a joke. Birdie has a plan. She won't tell me about it. Anyway, she says there's going to be money to run Lionnet and enough for me to borrow a little. I'll go on down to Brazil right away. Cod Carter says there's no trick in getting a commission with good pay. The planters there are looking for Confederate officers. I want to be with fighting men again. I'm lonely for them.

REGINA: Now you stop frightening me. I'm going to Chicago, and a month later you're coming and we'll get married. When Papa finds out he'll have a fit. Then we'll come on home for a while, and I'll talk him out of his fit—

JOHN, *gently, smiles:* Now you're joking. Don't talk silly, honey.

REGINA, *softly:* You don't want to come with me? You don't want to marry me?

JOHN, *after a second:* You don't ask that seriously.

REGINA, *softly:* Answer me, please.

JOHN: No. I don't. I never said I did. *Comes to her.* I don't want to talk this way, but I don't want to lie, either. Honey, I like you so much, but—I shouldn't have let us get like this. You're not in love with me. I'm no good for you—

REGINA: I am in love with you. I've never loved before, and I won't love again.

JOHN: My darling child, everybody thinks that, the first time. You're a lonely girl and I'm the first man you've liked. You can have anybody you want—

REGINA: John. Come away with me. We'll be alone. And after a while, if you still don't want me, then— *Softly:* I've never pleaded for anything in my life before. I might hold it against you.

JOHN: Oh, Regina, don't speak of pleading. You go away. By the time you come back, you'll be in love with somebody else, and I'll be gone.

REGINA, *stares at him:* Where did you say Miss Birdie was getting this money, this money for you to travel with?

JOHN: I don't know where: she won't tell me. But she says we'll have five thousand dollars this week.

REGINA, *after a second:* Five thousand?

JOHN, *nods:* I'd guess she's arranged something about

the Gilbert Stuart or the West. We haven't anything but the portraits—

REGINA: Is that what you'd guess? Well, I'd guess different. So she's planning to get you away from me?

JOHN: Nobody's *planning* anything. Oh, look, honey. This isn't any good. We'll go home now—

REGINA, *quickly, looking toward dining room:* Papa's coming. Please go in to supper now. It will be bad for me if you make any fuss or left now— *Softly:* We'll talk tomorrow. I love you. Go in to supper.

Marcus appears in the dining-room door.

JOHN, *who has his back to the door:* I'm sorry, honey, if— *He turns, moves across room, passes Marcus in the doorway, disappears into the dining room.*

Marcus stares at Regina; she does not look at him.

MARCUS: Who is sillier, who is more dead, the captain or his cousin? *She doesn't answer him.* You have a reason for not joining us at supper?

REGINA: I wanted to talk to—to Captain Bagtry.

MARCUS: Can he talk of anything but war?

REGINA: Have you agreed to make Ben's loan on Lionnet?

MARCUS: Ben's loan? Of course I'll make it. It is good for me, and bad for them. Got nothing to do with Ben.

REGINA: No? Have you asked yourself why Ben wants it so much?

MARCUS: I am not interested in Ben's motives. As long as they benefit me, he is welcome to them.

REGINA: How much money did he say Miss Birdie had asked for?

MARCUS: Ten thousand. *Regina smiles.* Why does this interest you?

REGINA, *rises:* Don't make the loan, Papa. I don't like the girl. I think she's come here tonight to make fun of us. She's snubbing all of us, laughing up her sleeve. Why should you pay her to do it?

MARCUS, *stares at her:* That's not true and I don't think you think it is. You're lying to me about something. Stop it. It hurts me. Tell me why you were talking to that man, why he called you honey—

REGINA, *carefully:* Ben is sometimes smarter than you are, and you are so sure he isn't, that you get careless about him. *Nods toward dining room.* Bagtry doesn't know about *your* loan on Lionnet, but the girl told him she was getting five thousand dollars this week. *Five thousand dollars, not ten.* I'd like to bet the extra five is meant for Ben to keep. *Carefully, as he stares at her:* You're getting older, Papa, and maybe you're getting tired and don't think as fast. I guess that happens to everybody. You'll have to start watching Ben even more—

MARCUS, *sharply:* All right, Regina.

Penniman and Jugger come in from the dining room.

They stand awkwardly, not knowing what to do. Regina goes into dining room.

PENNIMAN, *hesitates:* Shall we—would you like us to continue the music?

MARCUS: As soon as you have finished overeating.

Penniman coughs, embarrassed. Jugger starts forward angrily, then stops, follows Penniman out to the porch. Lavinia comes in from the dining room.

LAVINIA: I think that Miss Laurette has a touch of heart trouble. I asked the poor child what she was doing for it. She said she was trying to see if good, strong drinks would help. I've never heard that, although Ben says it's a good cure. She's a nice little thing.

MARCUS: You've always been a good judge of people, Lavinia, but that's true of all the pure in heart, isn't it?

Laurette, followed by Oscar, comes into the room. She is steady, but the liquor has blinded her a little, and she bumps into things. Oscar follows her, very nervous, staring at Marcus, who does not turn around.

LAVINIA, *speaks to Laurette only because she is nervous:* Hello.

Laurette now finds herself near the piano. She strikes a note. Pleased, she presses her right hand on the keyboard. Delighted, she presses both hands. Oscar jumps toward her.

LAURETTE: Hello . . . I never had opportunities . . . *Oscar grabs both her hands, she pulls them away, pounds again, grins, indicates Marcus:* Your Papa likes music, he says.

MARCUS, *to Oscar:* Is there any effective way of stopping that?

Laurette throws off Oscar, comes over to Marcus.

LAURETTE: Oskie says he wants to marry little old Laurette.

MARCUS: Does little old Laurette think that fortunate?

LAURETTE, *laughs—puts her hand through his arm:* Sometimes yes, sometimes no. We're going on down to New Orleans.

Ben and Birdie come in from the dining room.

MARCUS, *takes Laurette's hand from his arm:* This will sound very rude but I have a nervous dislike of being grabbed.

LAURETTE: Oh, sure. Me, too. Can't stand people pressing me unless I know about it, I mean. *Glares at Oscar:* Don't you ever press me, Oskie, unless I know about it.

MARCUS: That reminds me. I'm told you work for a living. That is good: Oscar is not a rich man.

LAURETTE, *laughs:* Rich? How could he be, on that stinking slave salary you pay him? That's why you're sure to repent and help us, Oskie says. When you die you're going to leave it to him anyway, so why not now, Oskie says?

MARCUS, *softly:* Oscar is a liar. Always has been. *Birdie moves toward porch.* And he steals a little. Nothing much, not enough to be respectable. But you know all that, of course.

Lavinia: Oh, Marcus. *Turns to Birdie:* My husband makes little jokes. All the time—

Oscar, *very loudly, to Marcus:* It's not true. It's just not true—

Marcus, *to Birdie:* Miss Bagtry, don't you find that people always think you're joking when you speak the truth in a soft voice?

Birdie, *very embarrassed:* No, sir. I—

Marcus, *back to Laurette:* If you want him, Miss Laurette, do have him.

Oscar, *with dignity:* Come on, Laurette. I'll settle this later.

Marcus laughs.

Laurette: Well, I'll just about say you will. A Papa talking about his son! No animal would talk about their own son that way. I heard tales about you ever since I was born, but—

Oscar, *frantic:* Come on, Laurette.

Laurette: You old bastard.

Marcus slowly rises.

Lavinia, *to Laurette:* Dear child—

Laurette, *to Marcus:* Everybody in this county knows how you got rich, bringing in salt and making poor, dying people give up everything for it. Right in the middle of the war, men dying for you, and you making their kinfolk give you all their goods and money—and I heard how they suspected you of worse, and you only just got out of a hanging rope. *Points to Oscar:* Why, the first night he slept with me, I didn't even want to speak to him because of you and your doings. My uncle used to tell me about—

BEN: Go on, Oscar. Get out.

John and Regina come in from dining room.

MARCUS, *to Oscar:* Take that girl out of here. Then come back. And come back quickly.

Oscar stares at him, starts to speak, changes his mind. Then he hurries to Laurette, takes her arm, moves her out. John crosses to Birdie.

LAVINIA, *in an odd tone:* Why, Marcus. The girl only told the truth. Salt is just a word, it's in the Bible quite a lot. And that other matter, why, death is also just a word. And—

MARCUS: You grow daring, Lavinia. *Moves toward her.* Now stop that prattling or go to your room—

BEN, *moves in front of him:* We have guests.

JOHN, *takes Birdie's arm, comes forward:* Good night and thank you, Mrs. Hubbard. *Coldly, to others:* Good night.

MARCUS: You came to beg a favor, and you stayed to be amused. Good night.

BIRDIE, *scared:* Mr. Hubbard, please . . .

JOHN: Came to ask a favor? From you? Who in this county would be so dishonored? If you were not an old man, Mr. Hubbard, I—

MARCUS: There is never so great a hero as the man who fought on a losing side.

BIRDIE, *goes to John—desperate:* Stop it, John. Go outside. Wait for me in the carriage.

JOHN: I don't want you here. Come on, Birdie—

BIRDIE, *firmly:* I want to stay for a few minutes. Please go outside. *Please. Please.*

He stares at her, then he turns, moves quickly out of the room. Marcus is watching Regina. Regina looks at Marcus, then turns and moves quickly after John. Marcus wheels around as if to stop Regina.

BIRDIE: Mr. Hubbard, I am sorry. John is upset. You know that his twin brother was killed that night in the massacre, and any mention of it—

MARCUS, *sharply:* What night do you speak of, Miss Birdie, and what massacre?

BIRDIE, *desperately:* Oh, I don't know. I—I'm just so sorry it has been unpleasant. I was hoping we could all be nice friends. Your family and mine—

MARCUS, *smiles:* Your mother hasn't bowed to me in the forty years I've lived in this town. Does she wish to be my nice friend now?

BIRDIE, *desperate:* Mama is old-fashioned. I'll speak to her and after a bit— *Pauses, looks down.* Oh. I've said the wrong thing again. I don't know how to— *Turns to him, simply:* I guess I just better say it simple, the way it comes to me. I didn't only come tonight for the loan. I *wanted* to come. I was frightened, of course, but, well, it was a big holiday for me, and I tried to get all dressed up in Mama's old things, and that was why we were late because I haven't had a new dress, and I've never had a party dress since I was four years old, and I had to get the dress without Mama's knowing why or where we were going, and I had to sew—

MARCUS: Then it *is* too bad you troubled yourself, because I have bad news for you: I have decided not to make the loan.

Birdie draws back, turns to Ben, starts to speak, puts her hands to her face.

BEN, *slowly:* Why? Why? You said yourself—

BIRDIE, *moves toward him:* Oh, please, Mr. Hubbard. Please. I went around all day telling our people they might be paid and—I'll give more, whatever you want—

MARCUS: That is unjust of you. I am not bargaining.

BEN, *angrily, to Marcus:* I want to know why you have changed your mind.

MARCUS: I will tell you, in time. *Turns to Birdie:* I am sorry to disappoint you. Please come another night, without a motive, just for the music.

BIRDIE: Yes, I had a motive. Why shouldn't I have? It was why I was asked here— Oh, I mustn't talk proud.

I have no right to. Look, Mr. Hubbard, I'll do anything. I'm sure you like good pictures: we have a Stuart and a West, and a little silver left. Couldn't I give—couldn't I bring them to you—

MARCUS, *gently, hurt:* Miss Birdie, Miss Birdie, please spare us both.

BIRDIE, *softly:* I was going to use the first money to buy molasses and sugar. All that land and cotton and we're starving. It sounds crazy, to need even molasses—

MARCUS: Everybody with cotton is starving.

BIRDIE, *angrily:* That's just a way of using a word. That isn't what I mean. I mean starving. *She looks up at him, her voice changes, sighs:* I should have known I couldn't do anything right. I never have. I'm sorry to have told you such things about us. You lose your manners when you're poor. *Goes to Lavinia:* Thank you, ma'am.

LAVINIA, *smiles gently, takes her hand:* Good night, child. You ride over and see me, or come down by the river and we'll read together.

BIRDIE, *smiles, crosses to Ben:* Thank you, Mr. Ben. I know you acted as my good friend.

MARCUS, *laughs:* Good night.

She nods, runs out.

LAVINIA, *after a second:* Goodness, Marcus. Couldn't you have—it's pig mean, being poor. Takes away your dignity.

MARCUS: That's correct, Lavinia. And a good reason for staying rich.

PENNIMAN'S VOICE: We're waiting for you, Mr. Hubbard.

MARCUS, *calling out:* That will be all for tonight.

Regina appears from the hall.

REGINA, *to Marcus:* I didn't intend you to insult them and make enemies of them.

MARCUS: Why are you so disturbed about the Bagtrys? *Ben laughs.* You are amused?

BEN: Yes. I am amused.

MARCUS: All right. Enjoy yourself—for a few minutes. *Penniman and Jugger appear carrying their instruments. Marcus turns to them:* The Mozart was carelessly performed. The carriage is waiting to take you to the station. Good night.

JUGGER: "Carelessly performed." What do you know about music? Nothing, and we're just here to pretend you do. Glad to make a little money once a month— *Angrily:* I won't do it any more, do you hear me?

MARCUS: Very well. Good night.

Jugger moves quickly out. Penniman comes forward, nervously.

PENNIMAN: He didn't mean—Gil is tired— Why, we're just as happy to come here— *No answer. Desperately:* Well, see you next month, sir. Just as usual. Huh?

When Marcus doesn't answer, Penniman sighs, exits as Oscar appears from porch.

OSCAR, *rushes toward Ben:* Trying to ruin my life, are you? Pouring liquor down her. Come on outside and fight it out like a man. I'll beat you up for it, the way you deserve—

LAVINIA, *as if she had come out of a doze:* Oh, goodness! The blood of brothers. *To Ben:* You in trouble, Ben? *Sees Oscar.* Oh, *you're* in trouble, Oscar.

OSCAR: Come on—

BEN: Oh, shut up.

Marcus laughs.

OSCAR, *turns on Marcus, angrily:* You laugh. I told you he had his eye on Birdie and Lionnet, and me getting it for him. So I fool him by bringing Laurette here. And then *he* fools *you:* gets Laurette drunk, and you get mad. That's just what he wanted you to do. And you did it for him. I think the joke's kind of on you.

REGINA: You must have told the truth once before in your life, Oscar, but I can't remember it.

MARCUS, *to Ben:* You're full of tricks these days. Did you get the girl drunk?

BEN: Just as good for Oscar to marry a silly girl who owns cotton, as a silly girl who doesn't even own the mattress on which she—

Oscar springs toward Ben, grabs his shoulder.

MARCUS, *to Oscar:* Will you stop running about and pulling at people? Go outside and shoot a passing nigger if your blood is throwing clots into your head.

OSCAR: I'm going to kill Ben if he doesn't stop—

MARCUS: Are you denying the girl makes use of a mattress, or do you expect to go through life killing every man who knows she does?

OSCAR, *screaming:* Papa, stop it! I am deeply and sincerely in love.

MARCUS: In one minute I shall put you out of the room. *Looks at Ben:* So that was the way it was supposed to work? Or better than that: the girl was to borrow ten thousand from me and you were to keep five of it, and take your chances on her being a fool, and nobody finding out.

BEN, *slowly:* I understand now. *Softly to Regina:* Bagtry told *you.* Yes? *Regina nods, smiles, sits down.*

MARCUS: Your tricks are getting nasty and they bore me. I don't like to be bored: I've told you that before.

BEN, *shrugs:* I want something for myself. I shouldn't think you were the man to blame me for that.

MARCUS: I wouldn't have, if you hadn't always been such a failure at getting it. *Goes to Ben:* I'm tired of your games, do you hear me? You're a clerk in my store and that you'll remain. You won't get the chance to try anything like this again. But in case you anger me once more, there won't be the job in the store, and you won't be here. Is that clear?

BEN, *slowly:* Very clear.

OSCAR, *who has been thinking:* Papa, you couldn't condemn a woman for a past that was filled with loathing for what society forced upon her; a woman of inner purity made to lead a life of outward shame?

MARCUS: What are you talking about?

REGINA: He's read a book.

MARCUS, *softly:* At nine years old I was carrying water for two bits a week. I took the first dollar I ever had and went to the paying library to buy a card. When I was twelve I was working out in the fields, and that same year I taught myself Latin and French. At fourteen I was driving mules all day and most of the night, but that was the year I learned my Greek, read my classics, taught myself— Think what I must have wanted for sons. And then think what I got. One unsuccessful trickster, one proud illiterate. No, I don't think Oscar's ever read a book.

LAVINIA: He did, Marcus. I used to read my Bible to him.

MARCUS, *to Oscar:* If you want to go away with this girl, what's detaining you?

OSCAR, *eagerly:* Your permission, sir.

MARCUS: Talk sense. Do you mean money?

OSCAR: Just a loan. Then we'd ship on down to New Orleans—

MARCUS: How much?

OSCAR: Could invest in a little business Laurette knows about— *Regina laughs loudly.* Ten thousand could start me off fine, Papa—

MARCUS: There will be a thousand dollars for you, in an envelope, on that table by six in the morning. Get on the early train. Send a Christmas card each year to an aging man who now wishes you to go upstairs.

OSCAR, *starts to protest, changes his mind:* Well, thank you. Seems kind of strange to be saying good-bye after twenty-five years—

REGINA, *gaily:* Oh, don't think of it that way. We'll be coming to see you some day. You'll have ten children, and five of the leaner ones may be yours.

LAVINIA: Good-bye, son. I'm sorry if— I'm sorry.

OSCAR: I'll write you, Mama. *To Ben, sharply:* You've bullied me since the day I was born. But before I leave—*fiercely*—you're going to do what I tell you. You're going to be on the station platform tomorrow morning. You're going to be there to apologize to Laurette.

MARCUS: Goodness, what a thousand dollars won't do!

OSCAR: And if you're not ready on time—*takes a pistol from his pocket*—I'll get you out of bed with this. And then you won't apologize to her standing up, but on your knees—

MARCUS, *violently, turning around:* Put that gun away. How dare you, in this house—

BEN, *smiles:* You've always been frightened of guns, Papa. Ever since that night, wasn't it?

LAVINIA: That's true, ever since that night.

MARCUS, *very angry: Put that gun away. And get upstairs. Immediately.*

OSCAR, *to Ben:* See you at the station. *He crosses room, exits.*

BEN, *after a second:* No need to be so nervous. I could have taken the gun away from him.

LAVINIA: And they had hot tar and clubs and ropes that night—

MARCUS: *Stop your crazy talk, Lavinia.*

LAVINIA, *softly:* I don't like that word, Marcus. No, I don't. I think you use it just to hurt my feelings.

BEN, *smiles:* He's upset, Mama. Old fears come back, strong.

MARCUS, *slowly, to Ben:* You're wearing me thin.

REGINA, *yawns:* Oh, don't you and Ben start again. *She pats Ben on the arm:* You know Papa always wins. But maybe you'll have your time some day. Try to get along, both of you. After Mama and I leave you'll be here alone together.

MARCUS: I don't know, darling. I'm going to miss you. I think I may join you.

REGINA, *turns, hesitantly:* Join me? But—

BEN: That would spoil the plan.

MARCUS, *to Regina:* I'll let you and Lavinia go ahead. Then I'll come and get you and we'll take a turn in New York. And then Regina and I will go on to Europe and you'll come back here, Lavinia.

LAVINIA: Oh, Marcus, you just can't have been listening to me. I been telling you since yesterday, and for years before *that*—

MARCUS, *looks at Regina:* You want me to come, darling?

REGINA, *nervously:* Of course. When were you thinking of coming, Papa? Soon or—

BEN, *to Regina—laughs:* I'm dying to see you get out of this one, honey.

MARCUS, *angrily, to Ben:* What are you talking about?

BEN: I'm going to be sorry to miss the sight of your face when Regina produces the secret bridegroom. *Marcus wheels to stare at Regina.* Oh, you know about it. You guessed tonight. Captain Bagtry. I don't think he wants to marry her. I don't think he even wants to sleep with her any more. But he's a weak man and— *Marcus is advancing toward him.* That won't do any good. I'm going to finish. Yesterday, if you remember,

Regina wanted you to make the loan to the girl. Tonight, when she found out John Bagtry wanted to use a little of the money to leave here, and her, she talked you out of it.

REGINA: *Ben, be still.* Ben— *Goes swiftly to Marcus:* Don't listen, Papa. I have seen John, I told you that. I like him, yes. But don't you see what Ben is doing? He wanted to marry me off to money, he's angry—

BEN, *to Marcus:* I'm telling the truth. The whole town's known it for a year.

LAVINIA: Don't, Benjamin, don't! Marcus, you look so bad—

BEN: You do look bad. Go up to him, Regina, put your arms around him. Tell him you've never really loved anybody else, and never will. Lie to him, just for tonight. Tell him you'll never get in bed with anybody ever again—

Marcus slaps Ben sharply across the face.

LAVINIA, *desperately:* God help us! Marcus! Ben!

BEN, *softly:* I won't forget that. As long as I live.

MARCUS: Lock your door tonight, and be out of here before I am down in the morning. Wherever you decide to go, be sure it's far away. Get yourself a modest job, because wherever you are, I'll see to it that you never get any other.

BEN: I spent twenty years lying and cheating to help make you rich. I was trying to outwait you, Papa, but I guess I couldn't do it. *He exits.*

LAVINIA: Twenty years, he said. Then it would be my fault, my sin, too— *She starts for hall door, calling:* Benjamin! I want to talk to you, son. You're my first-born, going away—

She disappears. There is a long pause. Marcus sits down.

MARCUS: How could you let him touch you? When did it happen? How could you— *Answer me.*

REGINA, *wearily:* Are they questions that can be answered?

MARCUS: A dead man, a foolish man, an empty man from an idiot world. A man who wants nothing but war, any war, just a war. A man who believes in nothing, and never will. A man in space—

REGINA, *softly—comes to him:* All right, Papa. That's all true, and I know it. And I'm in love with him, and I want to marry him. *He puts his hands over his face. She speaks coldly.* Now don't take on so. It just won't do. You let me go away, as we planned. I'll get married. After a while we'll come home and we'll live right here—

MARCUS: *Are you crazy?* Do you think I'd stay in this house with you and—

REGINA: Otherwise, I'll go away. I say I will, and you know I will. I'm not frightened to go. But if I go that way I won't ever see you again. And you don't want that: I don't think you could stand that. My way, we can be together. You'll get used to it, and John won't worry us. There'll always be you and me— *Puts her hand on his shoulder.* You must have known I'd marry some day, Papa. Why, I've never seen you cry before. It'll just be like going for a little visit, and before you know it I'll be home again, and it will all be over. You know? Maybe next year, or the year after, you and I'll make that trip to Greece, just the two of us. *Smiles.* Now it's all settled. Kiss me good night, darling. *She kisses him, he does not move. Then she moves toward door as Lavinia comes in.*

LAVINIA: Ben won't let me talk to him. He'd feel better if he talked, if he spoke out— I'm his Mama and I got to take my responsibility for what—

REGINA: Mama, I think we'll be leaving for Chicago sooner than we thought. We'll start getting ready to-morrow morning. Good night. *She exits.*

LAVINIA, *softly, after a minute:* Did you forget to tell her that I can't go with her? Didn't you tell them all where I'm going? I think you better do that, Marcus—

MARCUS, *softly—very tired:* I don't feel well. Please stop jabbering, Lavinia.

LAVINIA: You tell Regina tomorrow. You tell her how you promised me. *Desperately:* Marcus. It's all I've lived for. And it can't wait now. I'm getting old, and I've got to go and do my work.

MARCUS, *wearily:* It isn't easy to live with you, Lavinia. It really isn't. Leave me alone.

LAVINIA, *gently:* I know. We weren't ever meant to be together. You see, being here gives me—well, I won't use bad words, but it's always made me feel like I sinned. And God wants you to make good your sins before you die. That's why I got to go now.

MARCUS: I've stood enough of that. Please don't ever speak of it again.

LAVINIA: Ever speak of it? But you swore to me over and over again.

MARCUS: Did you ever think I meant that nonsense?

LAVINIA: But I'm going!

MARCUS: You're never going. Dr. Seckles knows how strange you've been, the whole town knows you're crazy. Now I don't want to listen to any more of that talk ever. I try to leave you alone, try to leave me alone. If you worry me any more with it, I'll have to talk to the doctor and ask him to send you away. *Softly—crying:* Please go to bed now, and don't walk around all night again.

LAVINIA, *stares at him:* Coralee. . . . Coralee! He never ever meant me to go. He says I can't go. Coralee— *She starts to move slowly, then she begins to run.* Coralee, are you in bed—

CURTAIN

Act Three

SCENE: *Same as Act One, early the next morning. At rise of curtain, Lavinia is moving about in the living room.*

LAVINIA, *singing:*

Got one life, got to hold it bold
Got one life, got to hold it bold
Lord, my year must come.

She comes on the porch. She is carrying a small Bible.

Got one life, got to hold it bold
Got one life, got to hold it bold
Lord, my year must come.

Ben, carrying a valise, comes from the living room. Lavinia gets up.

LAVINIA: All night I been waiting. You wouldn't let your Mama talk to you.

BEN: I put all my stuff in the ironing room. I'll send for it when I find a place.

LAVINIA, *softly:* Take me with you, son. As far as Altaloosa. There I'll get off, and there I'll stay. Benjamin, he couldn't bring me back, or send me, or do, or do. He couldn't, if you'd protect me for a while and—

BEN: I, protect you? *Smiles.* Didn't you hear him last night? Don't you know about me?

LAVINIA: I don't know. I heard so much. I get mixed. I know you're bad off now. *She reaches up as if to touch his face.* You're my first-born, so it must be my fault some way.

BEN: Do you like me, Mama?

LAVINIA, *after a second:* Well. You've grown away from— I loved you, Benjamin.

BEN, *turns away:* Once upon a time.

LAVINIA: Take me with you. Take me where I can do my little good. The colored people are forgiving people. And they'll help me. You know, I should have gone after that night, but I stayed for you children. I didn't know then that none of you would ever need a Mama. Well, I'm going now. *I tell you I'm going. Her voice rises.* I spoke with God this night, in prayer. He said I should go no matter. Strait are the gates, He said. Narrow is the way, Lavinia, He said—

BEN, *sharply:* Mama! You're talking loud. *Turns to her:* Go to bed now. You've had no sleep. I'm late. *Starts to move.*

LAVINIA: Take me, Benjamin!

BEN, *sharply:* Now go in to Coralee before you get yourself in bad shape and trouble.

LAVINIA: You've got to take me. Last night he said he'd never ever meant me to go. Last night he said if ever, then he'd have Dr. Seckles, have him, have him— *Turns, her fist clenched.* Take me away from here. For ten years he swore, for ten years he swore a lie to me. I told God about that last night, and God's message said, "Go, Lavinia, even if you have to tell the awful truth. If there is no other way, tell the truth."

BEN, *turns slightly:* The truth about what?

LAVINIA: I think, now, I should have told the truth that night. But you don't always know how to do things when they're happening. It's not easy to send your own husband into a hanging rope.

BEN: What do you mean?

LAVINIA: All night long I been thinking I should go right up those steps and tell him what I know. Then he'd have to let me leave or— *Puts her hands to her face.* I've always been afraid of him, because once or twice—

BEN: Of course. But you're not afraid of me.

LAVINIA: Oh, I been afraid of you, too. I spent a life afraid. And you know that's funny, Benjamin, because way down deep I'm a woman wasn't made to be afraid. What are most people afraid of? Well, like your Papa, they're afraid to die. But I'm not afraid to die because my colored friends going to be right there to pray me in.

BEN, *carefully:* Mama, what were you talking about? Telling the truth, a hanging rope—

LAVINIA: And if you're not afraid of dying then you're not afraid of anything. *Sniffs the air.* The river's rising. I can tell by the azalea smell—

BEN, *tensely, angrily:* For God's sake, Mama, try to remember what you were saying, if you were saying anything.

LAVINIA: I was saying a lot. I could walk up those steps and tell him I could still send him into a hanging rope unless he lets me go: I could say I saw him that night, and I'll just go and tell everybody I did see him—

BEN: *What night?*

LAVINIA: The night of the massacre, of course.

BEN, *tensely, sharply:* Where did you see him, how—

LAVINIA: You being sharp with me now. And I never been sharp with you. Never—

BEN, *carefully:* Mama. Now listen to me. It's late and there isn't much time. I'm in trouble, bad trouble, and you're in bad trouble. Tell me fast what you're talking about. Maybe I can get us both out of trouble. Maybe. But only if you tell me now. *Now.* And tell me quick and straight. You can go away and I—

LAVINIA, *rises:* I saw him, like I told you, the night of the massacre, on the well-house roof.

BEN: All right. I understand what you mean. All right. But there's a lot I don't know or understand.

Lavinia, *as if she hadn't heard him:* One time last night, I thought of getting his envelope of money, bringing it out here, tearing it up, and watching his face when he saw it at breakfast time. But it's not nice to see people grovel on the ground for money—

Ben: The envelope of money? The little envelope of money or the big envelope?

Lavinia: I could get it, tear it up.

Ben, *carefully:* Why not? Get it now and just tear it up.

Lavinia: And I thought too about giving it to the poor. But it's evil money and not worthy of the poor.

Ben: No, the poor don't want evil money. That's not the way.

Lavinia, *turns to him:* Oh, I am glad to hear you say that, but you can see how I have been tempted when I thought what the money could do for my little school. I want my colored children to have many things.

Ben, *desperately:* You can have everything for them if—

Lavinia: Oh, nobody should have everything. All I want is a nice school place, warm in winter, and a piano, and books and a good meal every day, hot and fattening.

Ben, *comes to her, stands in front of her:* Get up, Mama. Come here. He'll be awake soon. *Lavinia rises, he takes her by the arms.* Papa will be awake soon.

LAVINIA, *looks at him, nods:* First part of the war I was so ill I thought it was brave of your Papa to run the blockade, even though I knew he was dealing with the enemy to do it. People were dying for salt and I thought it was good to bring it to them. I didn't know he was getting eight dollars a bag for it, Benjamin, a little bag. Imagine taking money for other people's misery.

BEN, *softly:* Yes, I know all that, Mama. Everybody does now.

LAVINIA, *puzzled:* But I can't tell what you know, Benjamin. You were away in New Orleans in school and it's hard for me to put in place what you know and— *Ben moves impatiently.* So—well, there was the camp where our boys were being mobilized. It was up the river, across the swamp fork, back behind the old delta fields.

BEN: Yes, I know where it was. And I know that Union troops crossed the river and killed the twenty-seven boys who were training there. And I know that Papa was on one of his salt-running trips that day and that every man in the county figured Union troops couldn't have found the camp unless they were led through to it, and I know they figured Papa was the man who did the leading.

LAVINIA: He didn't lead them to the camp. Not on purpose. No, Benjamin, I am sure of that.

BEN: I agree with you. It wouldn't have paid him enough, and he doesn't like danger. So he didn't do it.

And he proved to them he wasn't here so he couldn't have done it. *Turns to her:* So now where are we?

LAVINIA: They were murder mad the night they found the poor dead boys. They came with hot tar and guns to find your Papa.

BEN, *softly:* But they didn't find him.

LAVINIA: But I found him. *She opens the Bible, holds it up, peers at it. Ben comes toward her.* At four-thirty o'clock Coralee and I saw him and heard him, on the well-house roof. We knew he kept money and papers there, and so we guessed right away where to look, and there he was.

BEN, *looks at her, smiles, softly:* And there he was.

LAVINIA: So you see I hadn't told a lie, Benjamin. He wasn't ever in the *house.* But maybe half a lie is worse than a real lie.

BEN, *quickly:* Yes, yes. Now how did he get away, and how did he prove to them—

LAVINIA: Coralee and I sat on the wet ground, watching him. Oh, it was a terrible thing for me. It was a wet night and Coralee caught cold. I had to nurse her for days afterward, with—

BEN, *looks up at balcony: Mama!* It's got to be quick now. Shall I tell you why? I've got to go unless— Now tell me how did he get away, and how did he prove to them that all the time he had been down Mobile road?

LAVINIA, *opens her Bible:* Twenty minutes to six he

climbed down from the roof, unlocked the well-house door, got some money from the envelope, and went on down through the back pines. Coralee and I ran back to the house, shivering and frightened. I didn't know what was going to happen, so we locked all the doors and all the windows and Coralee coughed, and sneezed, and ran a fever.

BEN, *angrily:* I don't give a damn about Coralee's health.

LAVINIA, *gently:* That's the trouble with you, Benjamin. You don't ever care about other folks.

There is the sound of a door closing inside the house.

BEN, *quietly: There is not much time left now. Try, Mama, try hard.* Tell me how he managed.

LAVINIA, *looks down at the Bible:* Well, three days later, no, two days later, the morning of April 5, 1864, at exactly ten-five—

BEN, *sharply:* What are you reading?

LAVINIA: He rode back into town, coming up Mobile road. They were waiting for him and they roped him and searched him. But he had two passes proving he had ridden through Confederate lines the day before the massacre, and didn't leave till after it. The passes were signed by—*looks at Bible*—Captain Virgil E. McMullen of the 5th Tennessee from Memphis. They were stamped passes, they were good passes, and they had to let him go. But he had no money when he came home. So Coralee and I just knew he paid Captain Virgil E.

McMullen to write those passes. *Looks down at book:* Virgil E. McMullen, Captain in the 5th Tennessee—

BEN, *tensely—points to Bible:* It's written down there?

LAVINIA: Coralee and I were half wild with what was the right thing to do and the wrong. So we wrote it all down here in my Bible and we each put our hand on the Book and swore to it. That made us feel better—

BEN: I'm sure of it. Give me the Bible, Mama—

LAVINIA: I think there's one in your room, at least there used to be—

BEN: Oh, Mama. For God's sake. I need it. It's the only proof we've got, and even then he'll—

LAVINIA: You don't need half this proof. That's the trouble with your kind of thinking, Benjamin. My, I could just walk down the street, tell the story to the first people I met. They'd believe me, and they'd believe Coralee. We're religious women and everybody knows it. *Smiles.* And then they'd want to believe us, nothing would give them so much pleasure as, as, as, well, calling on your Papa. I think people always believe what they want to believe, don't you? I don't think I'd have any trouble, if you stood behind me, and gave me courage to do the right talking.

BEN, *laughs:* I'll be behind you. But I'd like the Bible behind me. Come, Mama, give it to me now. I need it for us. *Slowly she hands the Bible to him.* All right. Now I'd like to have that envelope.

LAVINIA: But what has the money got to do with—I

don't understand why the envelope—I'm trying hard to understand everything, but I can't see what it has—

BEN: I can't either. So let's put it this way: it would make me feel better to have it. There's nothing makes you feel better at this hour of the morning than an envelope of money.

LAVINIA, *thinks:* Oh. Well. *Points into living room:* It's in the small upper left-hand drawer of your Papa's desk. But I don't know where he keeps the key.

BEN, *laughs:* That's very negligent of you. We won't need the key. *Takes her hand, takes her under balcony.* Now call Papa. I'll be back in a minute.

LAVINIA: Oh, I couldn't do that. I never have—

BEN, *softly:* You're going to do a lot of things you've never done before. Now I want you to do what I tell you, and trust me from now on, will you?

LAVINIA: I'm going to do what you tell me.

BEN, *goes into living room:* All right. Now go ahead.

Jake appears. He is carrying a mop and a pail.

JAKE: You all up specially early, or me, am I late?

LAVINIA, *calling:* Marcus. Marcus. *To Jake:* What do you think of that, Jake?

JAKE, *takes a nervous step toward her—softly:* I don't think well of it. Please, Miss Viney, don't be doing—

LAVINIA: Marcus! Marcus! I want—we want to speak

to you. *To Jake:* Hear what I did? *Nervously:* Everything's different—Marcus!

Marcus appears on the porch. He has been dressing; he is now in shirtsleeves. He peers down at Lavinia.

MARCUS: Are you shouting at me? What's the matter with you now, Lavinia?

LAVINIA: Well, I just—

MARCUS: You are up early to give your blessings to your departing sons?

LAVINIA: I haven't seen Oscar.

MARCUS: Benjamin has gone?

LAVINIA, *looks into drawing room:* No, Marcus. He hasn't gone. He's inside knocking off the locks on your desk. My, he's doing it with a pistol. The other end of the pistol, I mean.

During her speech, we hear three rapid, powerful blows. Marcus grips the rail of the porch. Ben comes onto the porch, the pistol in one hand, a large envelope in the other. He looks up at Marcus. There is a long pause.

MARCUS: Put the gun on the table. Bring me that envelope.

LAVINIA: Same old envelope. Like I said, I used to dream about tearing up that money. You could do it, Benjamin, right now. Make you feel better and cleaner, too.

BEN: I feel fine. *To Marcus:* I like you better up there. So stay there. *Stay there.* *Ben turns to Jake, takes an-*

other envelope from his pocket, puts in money from first envelope. Take this over to Lionnet. Ask for Miss Birdie Bagtry and talk to nobody else. Give her this and ask her to forget about last night.

MARCUS: Take that envelope from him, Lavinia, and bring it to me quickly.

LAVINIA: I can't walk as fast as I used to, Marcus, I'm getting old—

BEN, *to Jake:* Tell Miss Birdie I'll call on her in the next few days and we'll attend to the details then. Go on, be quick—

MARCUS, *to Jake:* Come back here! *To Ben:* How dare you touch—

BEN: Well, come and get it from me. *Turns again to Jake:* And tell her I wish Captain Bagtry good luck. And stop at the wharf and buy two tickets on the sugar boat.

LAVINIA: Thank you, son. *There is a long pause. She is puzzled by it.* Well. Why doesn't somebody say something?

BEN: We're thinking.

MARCUS: Yes. Shall I tell you what I'm thinking? That I'm going to be sorry for the scandal of a son in jail.

BEN: What would you put me in jail for?

MARCUS: For stealing forty thousand dollars.

BEN, *looking at the envelope, smiles:* That much? I haven't had time to count it. I always said there wasn't a Southerner, born before the war, who ever had sense enough to trust a bank. Now do you want to know what *I'm* thinking?

MARCUS: Yes, I'm puzzled. This piece of insanity isn't like you. In the years to come, when I do think about you, I would like to know why you walked yourself into a jail cell.

BEN: In the years to come, when you think about me, do it this way. *Sharply:* You had been buying salt from the Union garrison across the river. On the morning of April 2nd you rode over to get it. Early evening of April 3rd you started back with it—

MARCUS: Are you writing a book about me? I would not have chosen you as my recorder.

BEN: You were followed back—which is exactly what Union officers had been waiting for—at eleven o'clock that night—

LAVINIA: Marcus didn't *mean* to lead them back. I explained that to you, Benjamin—

MARCUS, *sharply:* *You* explained it to him? What—

BEN: Eleven o'clock that night twenty-seven boys in the swamp camp were killed. The news reached here, and you, about an hour later.

LAVINIA: More than that. About two hours later. Or maybe more, Benjamin.

MARCUS: What the hell is this? Lavinia, I want—

BEN: And the town, guessing right, and hating you anyway, began to look for you. They didn't find you. Because you were on the well-house roof.

LAVINIA: Yes you were, Marcus, that's just where you were. I saw you.

MARCUS, *softly:* I don't know why I'm standing here listening to this foolishness, and I won't be for long. Bring me the envelope, and you will still have plenty of time to catch the train. You come up here, Lavinia—

BEN: I'll tell you why you're standing there: you are very, very, very—as Mama would say—afraid.

MARCUS, *carefully:* What should I be afraid of, Benjamin? *Sharply:* A bungler who leaves broken locks on a desk to prove he's stolen, and gives away money to make sure I have further proof? Or a crazy woman, who dreams she saw something sixteen years ago?

LAVINIA: Marcus, I must ask you to stop using that awful word and—

MARCUS: And I must ask you to get used to it because within an hour you'll be where they use no other word—

BEN, *as Lavinia makes frightened motion:* Mama, stop it. *To Marcus:* And you stop interrupting me. Mama saw you on the well-house roof. Coralee saw you. They saw you take money from an envelope—

LAVINIA: The same one. My, it wore well, didn't it?

Ben: To buy the passes that saved you from a hanging. You bought them from—

Marcus, *tensely:* Get out of here. I—

Ben: From a Captain Virgil E. McMullen. Now I'd figure it this way: by the grace of Captain McMullen you got sixteen free years. So if they swing you tonight, tell yourself sixteen years is a long time, and lynching is as good a way to die as any other.

Lavinia: Benjamin, don't talk like that, don't, son—

Marcus, *in a different voice:* Walk yourself down to the sheriff's office now. I'll catch up with you. If you're fool enough to believe some invention of your mother's, understand that nobody else will believe it. The whole town knows your mother's been crazy for years, and Dr. Seckles will testify to it—

Ben: Let's put it this way: they think Mama is an eccentric, and that you made her that way. And they know Seckles is a drunken crook. They know Mama is a good woman, they respect her. They'll take her word because, as she told me a little while ago, people believe what they want to believe.

Marcus, *carefully:* Lavinia, you're a religious woman, and religious people don't lie, of course. But I know you are subject to dreams. Now, I wonder why and when you had this one. Remember, will you, that you were ill right after the incident of which you speak so incorrectly, and remember please that we took you—*sharply, to Ben*—not to that drunken Seckles, but to

Dr. Hammanond in Mobile. He told me then that you were— *Lavinia draws back.* And he is still living to remember it, if you can't.

LAVINIA, *worried, rattled:* I was ill after that night. Who wouldn't have been? It had nothing to do with, with my nerves. It was taking part in sin, your sin, that upset me, and not knowing the right and wrong of what to do—

MARCUS: She didn't tell you about that illness, did she? You think they'd believe her against Hammanond's word that she was a very sick woman at the time she speaks about? *Very sharply:* Now stop this damned nonsense and get out of here or—

BEN: Go change your dress, Mama. Get ready for a walk.

LAVINIA: But you told Jake—you said I could go on the sugar boat.

BEN: You can still catch the boat. We won't be walking long. And if you have to stay over a few hours more, I figure you can wear the same costume to a lynching as you can on a boat. We'll walk around to old Isham first, whose youngest son got killed that night. John Bagtry will be mighty happy to remember that his twin brother also died that night. And Mrs. Mercer's oldest son and the two Sylvan boys and— We won't have to go any further because they'll be glad to fetch their kinfolk and, on their way, all the people who got nothing else to do tonight, or all the people who owe you on cotton or cane or land. Be the biggest, happiest lynching in the history of Roseville County. All right. Go change your clothes—

MARCUS, *softly, carefully:* Lavinia. I—

LAVINIA: A lynching? *I don't believe in lynching.* If you lynch a white man, it can lead right into lynching a black man. No human being's got a right to take a life, in the sight of God.

MARCUS, *to Ben:* You're losing your witness. What a clown you turned out to be. Only you would think your mother would go through with this, only you would trust her—

BEN, *sharply:* She won't have to do much. I'm taking her Bible along. *Opens the book:* On this page, that night, she wrote it all down. The names, the dates, the hours. Then she and Coralee swore to it. Everybody will like the picture of the two lost innocents and a Bible, and if they don't, sixteen-year-old ink will be much nicer proof than your Mobile doctor. *Softly:* Anyway, you won't have time to get him here. Want to finish now?

LAVINIA, *who has been thinking:* I never told you I was going to have anything to do with a lynching. No, I didn't.

MARCUS: Of course you wouldn't. Of course you wouldn't. Not of your husband—

LAVINIA: Not of my husband, not of anybody.

BEN: Mama, go upstairs and let me finish this—

LAVINIA: I only said I was going to tell the truth to everybody. And that I'm going to do. *To Marcus:* If there's any nasty talk of lynching, I'm going to plead for your life hard as I can, yes I am.

BEN, *laughs:* Now, that's merciful of you. I'm going to do the same thing. I'm going to plead with them for Papa's life.

LAVINIA: That's the least a son can do for his father.

BEN, *to Marcus:* Better than that. I'll come tomorrow morning and cut you down from the tree, and bury you with respect. How did the Greeks bury fathers who were murdered? Tell me, and I'll see to it. You'd like that, wouldn't you?

LAVINIA: Benjamin, don't talk that way—

MARCUS: You gave him the right to talk that way. You did, Lavinia, and I don't understand anything that's been happening. Do you mean that you actually wrote a lie in your Bible, you who—

LAVINIA, *very angry:* Don't you talk like that. Nobody can say there's a lie in my Bible— You take that back. You take it back right away. I don't tell lies, and then I don't swear to them, and I don't swear on my Bible to a false thing and neither does Coralee. You just apologize to me and then you apologize to Coralee, that's what you do—

MARCUS, *quickly:* No, no. I don't mean you knew it was a lie. Of course not, Lavinia. But let me see it, and then tell me—

LAVINIA, *puts out her hand:* Let him see it. Of course.

BEN: Tell him to come down and look at it. I'll put it here, under the gun.

LAVINIA: Bibles are there for all people. For grown people. I'm not going to have any Bibles in my school. That surprise you all? It's the only book in the world but it's just for grown people, after you know it don't mean what it says. You take Abraham: he sends in his wife, Sarah, to Pharaoh, and he lets Pharaoh think Sarah is his sister. And then Pharaoh, he, he, he. Well, he does, with Sarah. And afterward Abraham gets mad at Pharaoh because of Sarah, even though he's played that trick on Pharaoh. Now if you didn't understand, a little child could get mighty mixed up—

MARCUS, *gently:* You want to go to your school, don't you, Lavinia?

LAVINIA: Or about Jesus. The poor are always with you. Why, I wouldn't have colored people believe a thing like that: that's what's the matter now. You have to be full grown before you know what Jesus meant. Otherwise you could make it seem like people ought to be poor.

BEN: All right. Go upstairs now and start packing. You're going to be on the sugar boat.

LAVINIA: Am I? Isn't that wonderful—

MARCUS: Lavinia. *She turns toward him.* It would be wrong of me to say ours had been a good marriage. But a marriage it was. And you took vows in church, sacred vows. If you sent me to trouble, you would be breaking your sacred vows—

BEN: Oh, shut up, Papa.

LAVINIA: I don't want trouble, for anybody. I've only wanted to go away—

MARCUS, *slowly, as he comes down from balcony:* I was wrong in keeping you.

BEN, *laughs:* Yes. That's true.

MARCUS: It was wrong, I can see it now, to have denied you your great mission. I should have let you go, helped you build you a little schoolhouse in Altaloosa.

BEN: I built it about ten minutes ago.

LAVINIA: What? Oh, about the marriage vows, Marcus. I had a message last night, and it said it was right for me to go now and do my work. Once I get a message, you know.

MARCUS: Yes. Yes, you'll want a lot of things for your colored pupils. A schoolhouse isn't enough—you'll need books and—

LAVINIA: That's absolutely true. And I want to send for a teacher— I'm getting old and I'm ignorant— I want to make a higher learning.

MARCUS: Lavinia. I'll get them for you.

LAVINIA: Thank you. But of course, it isn't just getting them, I've got to keep up the schoolhouse every year—

MARCUS: Certainly. Did your, did your messages suggest any definite figure?

LAVINIA: Why, yes, they did.

MARCUS: How much was suggested?

LAVINIA: To tell you the truth, my message said a thousand dollars a year would make my colored children happy. But I think ten thousand a year would make them happier. Altaloosa's a mighty poor little village and everybody needs help there—

MARCUS: Ten thousand wouldn't be enough. I think—

LAVINIA, *firmly:* It would be enough. I'd make it enough. Then, of course, I been forgetting about Coralee coming with me. And Coralee supports a mighty lot of kinfolk right here in town. She got a crippled little cousin, her old Mama can't take washing any more—

MARCUS: Oh, that's too bad. What could I do for them?

LAVINIA: Maybe two hundred dollars a month would take Coralee's mind from worrying.

MARCUS: I should think so. They'll be the richest family in the South. But, of course, your friends should have the best.

LAVINIA: You're being mighty nice to me, Marcus. I wish it had always been that way.

MARCUS, *quickly:* It started out that way, remember? I suppose little things happened, as they do with so many people—

LAVINIA: No, I don't really think it started out well. No, I can't say I do.

MARCUS: Oh, come now. You're forgetting. All kinds of pleasant things. Remember in the little house? The piano? I saved and bought it for you and—

LAVINIA: Bought it for me? No, I don't remember it that way. I always thought you bought it for yourself.

MARCUS: But perhaps you never understood why I did anything, perhaps you were a little unforgiving with me.

BEN, *to Marcus:* Aren't you getting ashamed of yourself?

MARCUS: For what? For trying to recall to Lavinia's mind that we were married with sacred vows, that together we had children, that she swore in a church to love, to honor—

BEN: If I wasn't in a hurry, I'd be very amused.

LAVINIA, *thoughtfully:* I did swear. That's true, I—

BEN, *quickly:* Mama, please go upstairs. Please let me finish here. You won't get on the boat any other way—

MARCUS: Indeed you will, Lavinia. And there's no need to take the boat. I'll drive you up. We can stay overnight in Mobile, look at the churches, have a nice dinner, continue on in the morning—

LAVINIA: How did you guess? I always dreamed of returning that way. Driving in, nice and slow, seeing everybody on the road, saying hello to people I knew as a little girl, stopping at the river church—church . . . *To herself:* Every Sunday here I always saved and put a dollar in the collection box. They're going to miss the dollar. You all know, in my vanity, what I'd like to have when I'm gone to Altaloosa?

MARCUS: What, Lavinia? I am most anxious to know.

LAVINIA: A mahogany pew, with my name on it, in brass.

MARCUS: Brass! It shall be writ in gold—

LAVINIA: I don't like gold. Brass. Now, what else did I think about last night?

MARCUS: We'll be in constant communication. And if you have more practical messages from God we can take care of them later. Now bring me the envelope and the Bible, and we'll start immediately—

She puts her hand on the Bible, as if to pick it up.

BEN, *quickly takes her hand:* Do I really have to explain it to you? Do I really have to tell you that unless you go through with it, he's got to take you to the hospital? You don't really think that he's going to leave you free in Altaloosa with what you know, to tell anybody— Why do you think he took you to Dr. Hammanond in the first place? Because he thought you might have seen him, and because it wouldn't hurt to have a doctor say that you were—

MARCUS, *very sharply:* That's a lie.

BEN: Maybe it is. But then you're only sorry you didn't think of it that way.

MARCUS: Lavinia—

LAVINIA, *softly:* I don't ever want to hear such things again, or one person do or say, to another.

MARCUS: Lavinia, you'll get what you want. You know I am not a stingy man or one who—

BEN: You'll get nothing. For the very simple reason that he isn't going to have a nickel to buy it with.

LAVINIA, *wearily:* Oh. That isn't what worries me— It's that Marcus may have been saying things he didn't mean. *Softly:* Would you really have told me you would drive me to Mobile and then you would have taken me—

MARCUS: *Of course not.* If you listen to that scoundrel— You're my wife, aren't you? I also took vows. I also stood up and swore. Would I break a solemn vow—

LAVINIA, *appalled:* Oh, now, I don't believe what you're saying. One lie, two lies, that's for all of us: but to pile lie upon lie and sin upon sin, and in the sight of God—

BEN, *sharply:* Write it to him, Mama. Or you'll miss your boat.

LAVINIA: Oh, yes. Oh, I wouldn't want to do that. *She picks up the Bible, exits.*

MARCUS: You're a very ugly man.

BEN: Are you ready now?

MARCUS: For what?

BEN: To write a piece of paper, saying you sell me the store for a dollar.

MARCUS, *pauses:* All right. Bring me that envelope. I'll sell you the store for a dollar. Now I have had enough and that will be all.

BEN: You'll write another little slip of paper telling Shannon in Mobile to turn over to me immediately all stocks and bonds, your safe-deposit box, all liens, all mortgages, *all* assets of Marcus Hubbard, Incorporated.

MARCUS: I will certainly do no such thing. I will leave you your proper share of things in my will, or perhaps increase it, if you behave—

BEN, *angrily:* You're making fun of me again. A will? That you could change tomorrow? You've made fun of me for enough years. It's dangerous now. One more joke. So stop it now. Stop it.

MARCUS: All right. But I would like to give you a little advice—you're so new at this kind of thing. If you get greedy and take everything there's bound to be a lot of suspicion. And you shouldn't want that. Take the store, take half of everything else, half of what's in the envelope. Give me the rest. I'll go on living as I always have, and tell everybody that because you're my oldest son, I wanted you to have—

BEN: You'll tell nobody anything, because you can't, and you'll stop bargaining. You're giving me everything you've got. Is that clear? If I don't have to waste any more time with you, I'll give you enough to live on, here or wherever you want to go. But if I have to talk to you any longer, you won't get that. I mean what I'm saying, and you know I do. And it's the last time I'll say it. *There is no answer. He smiles.* All right. Now start writing things down. When you finish, bring them to me. You're waiting for something?

MARCUS, *softly, as he goes up the porch steps:* To tell you the truth, I am trying to think of some way out.

BEN: If I told you that it's been a large temptation to see you—to do it the other way, you will believe me, I know; remember the past and don't waste your time, or put yourself in further danger, or tempt me longer. Ever since you started your peculiar way of treating me, many years ago, I have had many ugly dreams. But this is better than I ever dreamed— Go in and start writing now. I consider you a lucky man: you'll die in bed.

MARCUS: You will give me enough for a clean bed?

BEN: Yes, of course.

MARCUS: Well, I daresay one could make some small bargains with you still. But I don't like small bargains. You win or you lose—

BEN: And I don't like small talk. *Marcus turns, goes into his room. Ben waits for a second, then crosses to kitchen door, calls in:* Breakfast here, please. *As Jake comes from street side of porch:* Yes? Did you find Miss Birdie?

JAKE: Yes, sir. She was mighty happy and said to thank you.

BEN: All right. Did you get the tickets?

JAKE: Sure. Boat's loading now.

BEN, *sits down at Marcus's table:* Take them up to Miss Lavinia, get the carriage ready. Get me coffee first.

JAKE, *as he goes off:* Lot of running around this morning.

The sound of knocking is heard from the hall of the second floor.

OSCAR'S VOICE, *with the knocking:* Papa! Papa! It's me. Hey, Papa. Please. Open your door. *After a second Oscar runs in from the living room, runs up the porch steps, calls into Marcus's room:* Papa. I'm all ready. *Pounds on Marcus's door.*

BEN, *looking up at Oscar:* Traveling clothes? You look nice.

OSCAR: What you doing there? I told you to get on down to the station to make your apologies. I ain't changed my mind.

BEN: Oh, I never thought you meant that silly talk.

OSCAR: You didn't, huh? *Looks down, sees the gun on the table:* What's my pistol doing out?

BEN: Waiting for you.

OSCAR: You just put it back where you found it— *Then as if he remembered:* Papa. Please. Let me in. *Please.* Papa, I can't find it. Papa— *Regina appears on the balcony. She is arranging her hair. She has on a riding skirt and shirt.* Regina, go in and tell him, will you? *Please, Regina.* Laurette's waiting for me to fetch her up—

REGINA, *looks down at Ben on the porch. Looks at Oscar:* Oh, God. I slept late, hoping you'd both be gone. What's the matter with you, Oscar, what are you carrying on about?

Jake appears with coffee tray, brings cup to Ben, puts tray down, and exits.

OSCAR, *desperately:* The thousand dollars on the table. But it's *not* on the table. You heard him promise last night—

REGINA: Go look again. Papa certainly wouldn't stop your going.

OSCAR: I tell you it's not there. I been over the whole house. I crawled around under the table—

BEN: Come on down and crawl some more.

REGINA, *softly:* You're in Papa's chair, Ben, eating breakfast at Papa's table, on Papa's porch.

OSCAR, *softly, very puzzled:* I'm telling you that Ben is a crazy Mama's crazy son.

BEN, *looks up at Regina:* Come on down and have breakfast with me, darling. I'm lonely for you.

REGINA: Papa told you to be out of here.

BEN, *smiles:* Come on down, honey.

REGINA: No, I'm going out before the horse-whipping starts.

BEN: Going to look for a man who needs a little persuading?

REGINA: That's right.

OSCAR: Regina. Help me. It's *not* there. *Screaming:* Papa! *Papa!*

REGINA, *disappears into her room:* Oh, stop that screaming.

OSCAR: Papa, I got to go. The money's not there. Papa, please answer me—

MARCUS, *comes out from his room:* You looking for me, son? Speak up.

OSCAR, *softly:* It's getting late. The money. You forgot to leave it. *When he gets no answer, his voice changes to a sudden shriek:* It just ain't there.

MARCUS: A voice injured at your age is possibly never recovered. The money isn't there, Oscar, because I didn't put it there. *To Ben:* Would you like to give him a little—some—explanation, or will I, or—

BEN, *shakes his head:* I'm eating.

Oscar stares down at Ben, stares at Marcus.

MARCUS, *to Oscar:* An unhappy event interfered. I am thus unable to finance your first happy months in the rose-covered brothel about which you have always dreamed. I assure you I am most sorry, for many reasons, none of them having anything to do with you.

OSCAR: What the hell does all that mean? That you're *not* giving me the money to leave here—

BEN, *nods:* It means that. And it means that Papa has found a new way of postponing for a few minutes an unpleasant writing job. Go back in, Papa.

Oscar stares at Marcus, stares down at Ben. Then he suddenly runs down the steps, off the porch, going toward the street. Ben smiles, Marcus smiles.

MARCUS: Where would you prefer me to have breakfast? A tray in my room, this side of the porch, or the dining room or—

BEN: Any place you like. My house is your house.

MARCUS: I eat a large breakfast, as you know. Should that continue?

BEN: Certainly. But before you eat this large breakfast, on this large morning, I want you to finish the papers I'm waiting for.

MARCUS: Naturally, I've been inside thinking. Is there any chance I could get out of here and on the train without your interfering with me?

BEN: No, I don't think so. I've thought of that. And if you did, I feel confident I could bring you back.

MARCUS, *pleasantly:* Yes. Thank you, Benjamin.

He re-enters his room as Regina comes on the porch. She hears his last sentence, stares at Marcus. She comes down the steps, goes to the table, pours herself coffee, takes a biscuit, looks curiously at Ben and sits down.

REGINA, *after a minute:* What's the matter with Papa?

BEN: He's changed. You think it's age?

REGINA, *annoyed:* Why aren't you getting on the train?

BEN: I'm going to build a new house. I never liked this house; it wasn't meant for people like us. Too delicate, too fancy. Papa's idea of postwar swell.

REGINA, *stares at him:* I want to know why you aren't leaving this morning?

BEN: I can't tell you why. *Laughs.* My lips are sealed in honor.

REGINA: Before there's any more trouble you better go quiet down Mama. She's *packing.* She says she's going to her destiny. You know what that always means. And I'm sick of fights—

BEN: But that's where she is going.

REGINA, *bewildered:* Papa said she could go?

BEN: No . . . I said so.

REGINA: And who have you become?

BEN: A man who thinks you have handled yourself very badly. It's a shame about you, Regina: beautiful, warm outside, and smart. That should have made a brilliant life. Instead, at twenty, you have to start picking up the pieces, and start mighty fast now.

REGINA, *gets up, laughs:* I like the pieces, and I'm off to pick them up.

BEN: To try to persuade the Captain by the deed of darkness to a future legal bed? So early in the morning?

REGINA, *pleasantly, as she passes him:* I'm sure something very interesting has happened here. *Sharply. Turns to him:* But whatever it is, don't talk that way to me.

BEN: Can I talk this way? You're not going to Chicago. And for a very simple reason. Papa has no money at all—now. No money for you to travel with, or to marry with, or even to go on here with.

REGINA, *stands staring at him. Then, quietly: What are you talking about? What's happened?* What's he done with his money—

BEN: Given it to me.

REGINA: Do you take that new drug I've been reading about? What would make you think he had given it to you?

BEN: You mean what were his reasons? Oh, I don't know. I'm the eldest son: isn't that the way with royalty? Maybe he could find me a Greek title— Go up and talk to him. I think he's been waiting.

Slowly she starts for the staircase. Then the speed of her movements increases, and by the time she is near the door of Marcus's room she is running. She goes into the room. Ben picks up his newspaper. There is low talk-

ing from Marcus's room. Ben looks up, smiles. After a moment, Regina comes slowly out of Marcus's room. She crosses porch, starts downstairs.

REGINA, *slowly:* He says there is nothing he will tell me. He says there's nothing he can tell me. He's crying. What does all that mean?

BEN: It means there is nothing he can tell you, and that he's crying. Don't you feel sorry for him?

REGINA: Why can't he tell me? I'll make him—

BEN: He can't tell you, and I won't tell you. Just take my word: you're, er, you're not well off, shall we say?

REGINA, *tensely:* What have you been doing to Papa or—

BEN: A great deal. Whatever you think of me, honey, you know I'm not given to this kind of joke. So take it this way: what is in your room, is yours. Nothing else. And save your time on the talk. No Chicago, honey. No nothing.

REGINA: You can't stop my going, and you're not going to stop it—

BEN: Certainly not. What people want to do, they do. You go ahead, your own way. Ride over to your soldier. Stand close and talk soft: he'll marry you. But do it quickly: he was angry last night and I think he wants to get away from you as fast as he can. Catch him quick. Marry him this morning. Then come back here to pack your nice Chicago clothes, and sell your pearls.

REGINA: Do you think I'm going to take your word for what's happening, or believe I can't talk Papa out of whatever you've done to him—

BEN: Believe me, you can't. Not because your charms have failed, but because there's nothing to talk him out of. I have it now, and your charms won't work on me. Money from the pearls will be plenty to take you to Brazil, and love and war will feed you. People in love should be poor.

REGINA: Ben, tell me what storm happened here this morning. Tell me so that I can—can find out what I think or—

BEN: Or if you don't want to go to the war in Brazil, stay here and starve with them at Lionnet. I'd love to see you in the house with those three ninnies, dying on the vine. Either way, he'd leave you soon enough and you'd find out there's never anybody nastier than a weak man. Hurry— Or have a cup of coffee.

REGINA, *softly, tensely:* I'll find out what's happened, and—

BEN: No you won't.

REGINA: And the day I do, I'll pay you back with carnival trimmings.

BEN: Good girl. I won't blame you. But in the meantime, learn to win, and learn to lose. And don't stand here all day losing, because it's my house now, and I don't like loser's talk.

REGINA: You've ruined everything I wanted, you've—

BEN: Now, look here. Write *him* a poem, will you? I've ruined nothing. You're not marrying a man who didn't love you. You can't go away, or at least not on my money, and therefore a willful girl can't have a willful way. You're not in love; I don't think anybody in this family can love. You're not a fool; stop talking like one. The sooner you do, the sooner I'll help you.

REGINA: You heard me say I'd pay you back for this?

BEN: All right. Be a fool.

Marcus opens his door, comes out on the porch, comes down the steps. Regina turns to look at him. Marcus comes to Ben, hands him two pieces of paper. Ben takes them, reads them. Marcus puts his hand out to take the newspaper. Ben smiles, shakes his head, Marcus quickly takes his hand away.

REGINA, *desperately, to Marcus:* You still won't tell me? You're willing to see—

MARCUS, *softly:* Regina, honey, I can't, I—

Oscar, dejected and rumpled, appears.

REGINA, *to Oscar:* Do you know what's happened here? Did you have anything to do with it?

OSCAR: What?

Regina turns away from him. Oscar sits down, puts his head in his hands.

REGINA, *after a minute:* Well, what's the matter with you then? Ben Hubbard trouble?

OSCAR: She wouldn't wait. She wouldn't even wait for a few days until Papa could give me the money again.

BEN: Again?

OSCAR: That's how much she cared for me. Wouldn't even wait. Said she was going on to New Orleans, anyway. That she'd had enough— My God, I talked and begged. I even tried to carry her off the train.

MARCUS: Oh, how unfortunate.

BEN: I think it's charming. How did you do it, Oscar?

OSCAR, *to nobody:* You know what she did? She spat in my face and screamed in front of everybody that she was glad I wasn't coming, that she had never cared for me, and had only been doing the best she could. If I didn't have the money, what the hell did she need me for?

REGINA, *sympathetic:* Spat in your face! How could she do a thing like that?

MARCUS: How does one spit in your face?

BEN: Why, I imagine the way one spits in anybody's face.

REGINA: But it's special in a railroad station. How did she do it, Oscar? You can't just up and spit—

OSCAR, *in his sorrow, spits out on the porch:* Just like that. The way you wouldn't do with a dog. And all the while yelling I was to let her alone, with everybody staring and laughing— *Marcus, Regina, and Ben laugh. Oscar rises.* So. So, making fun of me, huh?

REGINA: Now, really, Oskie, can you blame us? You on a railroad station trying to carry off a spitting—girl? You'd laugh yourself, if you didn't always have indigestion.

OSCAR, *carefully:* Your love didn't laugh. Your love, looking like a statue of Robert E. Lee. Dressed up and with his old medals all over him. *Regina rises. Marcus rises.* So you didn't know he was going on the train, huh? I thought not. So you're no better off than me, are you, with all your laughing. Sneaked out on you, did he?

REGINA: So you arranged that, too, so that I couldn't—

BEN: All right. That's enough. I'm sick of love. Both of you follow the trash you've set your hearts on, or be still about it from now on. I don't want any more of this.

OSCAR: *You* don't want any more. What the—

BEN, *to Regina:* You, early-maturing flower, can go any place you want and find what it's like to be without Papa's money. *To Oscar:* And you, lover, can follow your spitting heart and get yourself a wharf job loading bananas. Or you can stay, keep your job, settle down. I got a girl picked out for you—make yourself useful.

OSCAR, *completely bewildered, turns to Marcus:* What's he talking about, Papa? Since when—

BEN: It's not necessary to explain it to you. *To Regina:* Now, honey, about you, if you're staying. You're a scandal in this town. Papa's the only person didn't know you've been sleeping with the warrior.

MARCUS: Benjamin—

BEN, *laughs:* Papa, and Horace Giddens in Mobile. How soon he'll find out about it, I don't know. Before he does, we're taking you up to see him. You'll get engaged to him by next week, or sooner, and you'll get married in the first church we bump into. Giddens isn't bad off, and if you're lucky it'll be years before he hears about you and the Brazilian general. I don't say it's a brilliant future, but I don't say it's bad. You could have done a lot better, but girls who have been despoiled in this part of the country—

MARCUS, *softly:* You don't have to marry a man, Regina, just because— We can go away, you and I—

OSCAR, *goes toward kitchen door:* I certainly don't know what's happened here. I certainly don't. I'm hungry. *Calls in:* Where's breakfast, you all?

REGINA, *sharply:* Order breakfast for me, too, selfish.

BEN, *laughs:* That's my good girl. *Picks up the newspaper.* Nothing for anybody to be so unhappy about. You both going to do all right. I'm going to help you. I got ideas. You'll go to Chicago some day, get everything you want— Then—

REGINA, *softly:* When I'm too old to want it.

MARCUS: Regina, you didn't hear me. We could go away, you and I— I could start over again just as I started once before.

REGINA: When you did—whatever Ben made you do, did you realize what you were doing to me? Did you care?

MARCUS, *slowly:* I cared very much.

REGINA: And what good did that do?

OSCAR: Sure must have been an earthquake here since last night. You go to bed and Papa's one kind of man, and you wake up—

BEN, *reading newspaper:* They got that ad in again, Oscar. Dr. Melgoyd's "All Cure." Two bits, now, on special sale, for gentlemen only. Sluggish blood, cure for a wild manhood, nothing to be ashamed of, it says—

REGINA: He's still got the last bottle.

Jake appears with a large tray. He has on his hat and coat.

OSCAR, *annoyed:* I never bought that rot. Don't believe in it. Somebody gave it to me.

REGINA, *laughing:* That was tactless, wasn't it?

BEN: Big goings on all over the country. Railroads going across, oil, coal. I been telling you, Papa, for ten years. Things are opening up.

OSCAR, *who has started to eat:* That don't mean they're opening up in the South.

BEN: But they are. That's what nobody down here sees or understands. Now you take you, Papa. You were smart in your day and figured out what fools you lived among. But ever since the war you been too busy getting cultured, or getting Southern. A few more years and you'd have been just like the rest of them.

MARCUS, *to Jake:* Bring my breakfast, Jake.

JAKE: Belle will have to do it, Mr. Marcus. Last breakfast I can bring. I got the carriage waiting to take Miss Viney. *He exits.*

BEN: But now we'll do a little quiet investing, nothing big, because unlike Papa I don't believe in going outside your class about anything—

OSCAR, *his mouth full:* Think we've got a chance to be big rich, Ben?

BEN: I think so. All of us. I'm going to make some for you and Regina and—

Lavinia appears in the living-room door. She is carrying a purse and the Bible. Coralee is standing behind her.

LAVINIA: Well, I'm off on my appointed path. I brought you each a little something. *Goes to Regina:* This is my pin. *Regina gets up, Lavinia kisses her.* Smile, honey, you're such a pretty girl. *Goes to Oscar:* Here's my prayer book, Oscar. I had it since I was five years old. *Oscar kisses her. She goes to Ben:* I want you to have my Papa's watch, Benjamin.

BEN: Thank you, Mama. *He kisses her, she pats his arm.*

LAVINIA, *goes to Marcus:* I didn't have anything left, Marcus, except my wedding ring.

MARCUS, *gets up, smiles:* That's kind, Lavinia.

LAVINIA: Well, I guess that's all.

BEN: Mama, could I have your Bible instead of Grandpa's watch? *Marcus laughs.* It would make me happier, and I think—

MARCUS: Or perhaps you'd give it to me. I can't tell you how happy it would make me, Lavinia.

LAVINIA: Oh, I wouldn't like to give it up. This Bible's been in my Papa's family for a long time. I always keep it next to me, you all know that. But when I die, I'll leave it to you all. Coralee, you hear that? If I die before you, you bring it right back here.

CORALEE: Come on, Miss Viney.

LAVINIA: I'll be hearing from you, Benjamin?

BEN: You will, Mama. Every month. On time.

LAVINIA: Thank you, son. Thank you in the name of my colored children.

CORALEE: Miss Viney, it's late.

LAVINIA: Well. *Wistfully:* Don't be seeing me off, any of you. Coralee and I'll be just fine. I'll be thinking of you, and I'll be praying for you, all of you. Everybody needs somebody to pray for them, and I'm going to pray for you all. *Turns to Marcus:* I hope you feel better, Marcus. We got old, you and me, and— Well, I guess I just mean it's been a long time. Good-bye.

MARCUS: Good-bye, Lavinia.

Lavinia and Coralee exit. Marcus goes to sit by Regina.

MARCUS, *softly:* Pour me a cup of coffee, darling.

Regina looks at him, gets up, crosses to table, pours coffee, brings it to him. Marcus pulls forward the chair next to him. Regina ignores the movement, crosses to chair near Ben, sits down. Ben smiles.

CURTAIN FALLS